Cecilia Tan

THE MYSTERY OF THE BITTEN PEACH

Neon Hemlock Press

NEON HEMLOCK

Neon Hemlock Press
www.neonhemlock.com
@neonhemlock

© 2026 Cecilia Tan

The Mystery of the Bitten Peach
Cecilia Tan

Cover Illustration by Jenn So
Interior Design and Layout by dave ring
Edited by dave ring

Print ISBN-13: 978-1-966503-24-8
Ebook ISBN-13: 978-1-966503-25-5

THE MYSTERY OF THE BITTEN PEACH

———

CECILIA TAN

For Aunt Reenie

Distance tests a horse's heart.
Time tests a human's.

(Chinese proverb)

SOME STORIES ARE day stories, full of hope and the promise of renewal that comes with the dawn. Some stories are night stories, full of mystery and shadow and desires unspoken, brought on by the dusk. I still don't know which kind my story is.

Given *me*, perhaps it's both.

And either way, I should have let it get closer to daybreak before taking those jade earrings. Now I'm weaving from building to building in the compound, dodging an army of footmen with lanterns, some paper, some silk, all in fervent pursuit. My Chinese history class never taught me lanterns came in so many shapes.

My Chinese history class never taught me a lot of things.

The estate is large, and as more and more of the governor's men join the search for the thief, the one thing saving me is their assumption I must be trying to make it to the outer wall, to escape and disappear into the city to the west, or the foothills to the east. They think that if they guard the edges of the compound, the barriers built to keep other people *out* will keep me *in*.

They're wrong...I hope. I duck into a dark alcove, hoping to go unseen at least a little longer. The last gong of the night already sounded, but either I converted the time wrong or it's overcast—or both—because the sky is still black. Part of me wants to try without waiting for daybreak, but...maybe I shouldn't rush, since that didn't work out so well last time. The shouting and rattling of weapons recedes, leaving the corridor nearly silent. For the moment the uproar has passed me by.

I can't stand to wait anymore. I step through the archway into an inner courtyard—a contemplation garden with curiously shaped rocks taller than a horse. Above me, I can barely make out layers of cloud sliding past one another like long lizards on a riverbank and, *there!* Where they part, a sliver of crimson light appears like a baleful eye peeking open. A startled cock crows and surely that is the most auspicious sign it is time for me to go. I center myself with a breath, and turn to find the doorway behind me fragmenting like infinite mirrors within mirrors. Yes, here we go.

I clutch the earrings inside my pocket, one last pang of worry tightening the spot between my shoulders. I'd hoped to slip away totally unnoticed—the theft *could* have gone undetected for days or weeks. Now, though, will they search the city? Will some fence get his hands broken for telling the truth: he's never seen me or the earrings? Or maybe I am just being dramatic. Maybe nothing will come of it but a petulant plea to the governor from his mistress to replace them.

I turn my thoughts from the past to the future—though for me it is always the present. I step through the doorway and into the kaleidoscope that is my domain. My foot comes down in a familiar alley, and I lean in relief against the brick of a doorway I know. The air smells like New York, like steam, and rot, and tar. I am at the delivery entrance in the back of Quan's antique shop, and it is sunset.

The back door is propped open to let the summer evening air into the cramped little shop, the screendoor latched lightly by a hook.

Perfect. I ring the bell.

I hear his grumbling before I see him, griping about delivery drivers in a dialect I recognize but don't speak. He breaks into a grin and switches to English the moment he realizes it's me.

"Mei-Mei!" That's what he calls me. "Back so soon?" He looks worried for a moment.

"I got what you asked for," I reassure him, and he hurries me inside before I can say anything more. We hold some secrets between us and I suppose I can't blame him for wanting to keep it that way.

He leads me through a storeroom so crammed that there's only a winding, narrow path between the stacks, shelves, and heaps. I don't even know what all that stuff is, and if I ask, I know Quan will say "Antiques!" and then laugh his head off. The front of the shop isn't much better, but at least the counter is clear and there would be room for a few customers to walk around—if there ever were customers. I can't say I've ever seen any. Quan flips over the sign in the window that says *closed* in several languages and throws the deadbolt.

He starts the electric kettle next to the cash register and is startled by the sound of a phone ringing inside the pocket of his jacket. He pulls out the handset of a cordless phone and says "Wey?" but the phone rings again: the cell phone in his other pocket. He sighs and switches devices; the annoyance disappears from his voice as soon as he picks it up. "Ahhh! Can I call you back? I'm in a meeting." He laughs at whatever the person on the other end says, or maybe just at the idea of actually being "in a meeting." I get the feeling most of what Quan does all day is crossword puzzles.

The grin remains on his face as he hangs up and fetches his loupe. "You'd think I would be used to mobile phones by now."

"I'm not used to them yet, either," I say, letting out a long breath as I place the earrings on a leather pad in front of him.

He looks up from examining the jade treasures and examines me instead. "Are you all right?"

"I'm fine. A bit of a close call at the end." My heart is still beating hard. I am a thousand years away from the trouble, even if it was only a few minutes ago from my perspective. "No big deal."

He gives me a skeptical glare and sweeps the earrings into a pouch and out of sight. He punches something into the cash register to open the drawer. Before he hands the money over, though, he says, "Are you interested in a more difficult job?"

"Might depend on what you mean by 'more difficult.'"

"I will explain over tea."

Quan seems to feel tea is necessary—if not an entire multi-course meal—to have any conversation longer than a minute. I try to forestall him. "What's different this time?"

"It's for a very...prestigious institution." He handles his words as if they are as fragile as the thimble-sized cups of porcelain he sets on the counter between us. "A museum."

I find myself intrigued. He's never told me anything about who I'm retrieving things for. "Why does it matter?"

"Because this one's magical." He lifts the kettle before it can fully boil. "And it's missing."

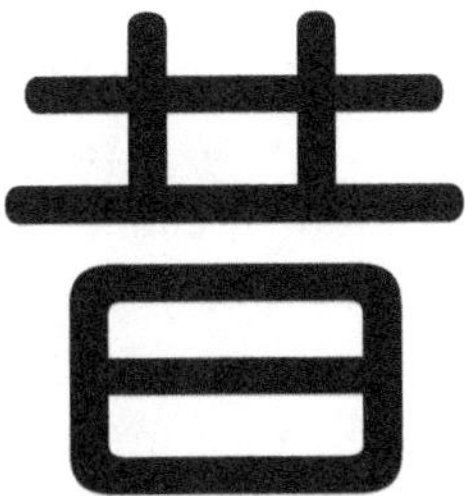

WASN'T ALWAYS A time-traveling thief. I was raised in the Midwest, mostly Ohio, the only child of a doctor and his wife. I have no memories of him other than the mantelpiece of photographs my mother kept after he died when I was still too young to know him. He was Chinese, she was white. When my mother and I went anywhere together she would get horribly offended if anyone asked if I was adopted—and they frequently would. I remember being young enough to ask why people would think that and her telling me that it was because I "took after" my father.

I had thought she acted so offended because I was her flesh and blood. She didn't tell me I was actually adopted from the mainland until I was sixteen. By then I'd had years of feeling like a duckling being raised by a swan: the knowledge came as a strange kind of relief. I had so many questions, but the one I actually asked was why had she waited so long to tell me?

And she had answered, "It was never the right time." Funny, right?

After that, I felt less and less connected to a place where I'd never fit in, and I left for college in a big city. There, I had twelve weeks of a Chinese history course and six months of morning Mandarin classes, but whatever I was looking for, I didn't find in them, either. When I told her I wasn't coming home for the summer, she objected, but it's not like she could really force me to come back. She would've been so horrified by my actual plan for that summer that I didn't even tell her what I'd be doing: I'd gotten a job in Chinatown. I ended up stringing a few jobs together, slinging steamed buns at a bakery for a few weeks, answering the phone and taking orders at a takeout joint for a few more, eventually landing a position as a bar hostess at one of the big dim sum palaces, even though I wasn't yet old enough to drink.

I wasn't prepared at all for what I found there. Picture me running up the stairs while Skinny Dou (who wasn't skinny at all) screamed at me in at least two languages to go upstairs and make myself pretty for the customers. I burst into a room and found the most beautiful woman I'd ever seen standing at a plate glass window watching the sun set over the city, so still she could've been a Tang Dynasty statue. I stared, not daring to move, until she turned and smiled and began trying on different dialects until we hit on enough common words and gestures to understand each other a little. I gleaned that she would help me with my hair and clothing, and I would help with hers. She was already wearing a traditional-looking outfit, but her hair was loose and long. She pressed a green and black high-collared cheung-sam at me, nowhere near so fine as hers, and urged me to try it on.

The sun met the horizon, casting a rectangle of gold across the ceiling, and my eyes kept flicking to the door. Skinny Dou or anyone else might come through it at any moment. I had no way to argue, so I pushed a chair in front of the door, kicked off my sneakers and peeled out of my T-shirt and jeans.

She told me to call her Jin Jin, but none of my names would fit in her mouth.

She was the one who named me Mei.

今

THEY SAY THE first step in solving a mystery is to visit the scene of the crime. I head uptown to the Metropolitan Museum of Art, where I skirt the throngs trying to see whatever the latest big exhibition is, and make my way to the gallery of Asian Art. A stone Buddha towers atop a wide marble staircase, serenely dominating the space.

The main collection is varied and large, mostly kept in glass cases. A year ago I would barely have known what I was seeing, but my jaunts into the past have made many things more real to me.

And hey, that bowl from the Five Dynasties period looks *very* familiar.

Next to it stands an empty case with plywood replacing a broken pane. The placard, though, is still here.

Jade, China, (540 bce)
sculpted representation of "the bitten peach"

Based upon the folktale of Duke Ling of Wei and his male lover, the viscount Mizi Xia, this sculpted piece represents the pinnacle of the jade carvers' art in the early Qing dynasty. According to the tale, the two men were walking through the royal garden, and the viscount spied a low-hanging peach. He plucked the peach and in his sensual bliss after having bitten it, offered it to his lover to share. The duke was so moved by the intimacy inherent in the gesture that he said: "He loves me to the point of forgetting his own mouth and giving it to me!" Later, however, when the viscount lost his beauty, the duke renounced their relationship. It is not known whether the story is true, but homosexuality is still referred to in China as the "pleasure of the bitten peach."

"Sad, isn't it?"

I startle. Next to me is an Asian-looking woman in a smart skirt-and-jacket ensemble, her hair in a bun and a museum employee name tag on her lapel. I pretend I haven't been startled. "Er, sad?"

"Yes, that the Duke could be so fickle." A single click of her heel against the marble floor punctuates the step she takes toward me. "Not to mention that the current regime would like to purge any knowledge of gay history."

The way she looks at me over the tops of her glasses, appraising me, makes my throat dry and my mouth unstoppable: "You think that's who took it?" I blurt.

A small smile appears. "You must be Mei Song."

Am I? I suppose Quan gave me a last name for credibility's sake. I've certainly never told him any family name. "Yes. Quan sent me."

I wipe my hands on my jeans before shaking the cool, smooth hand of Sandra Lim, curator. We were supposed to meet at her office at two o'clock, but I suppose now will do.

Her lips are seashell pink and I'm trying not to stare at them as she speaks. "Quan and I are old friends."

For a moment I wonder if she means old-old, but when I let my eyes go soft, she fades into the background like every other person nearby. She doesn't have the luminous, *permanent* quality that the immortals do. What she does have is an unexpected measure of self-possession, and strangely warm, reddish-brown eyes. I wonder if she's part Caucasian, but when I don't want people prying into my background, I don't pry into theirs.

Whatever she is, I feel like an uncouth puppy next to her.

"We can talk more in my office, if you like."

"Of course." I heel far too eagerly and I know it.

I ALMOST KISSED A girl when I was fifteen. She was thirteen, but she was already far more sophisticated than I was, in an especially feminine way: her red hair curled, her nails painted. She had just moved into the house across the street and was due to start at my school in September. Our mothers conspired that we should socialize together that summer since she had not yet made any friends in her own grade.

My mother in particular thought this girl could teach me something about how to dress, how to behave. Normally I resisted any attempt to feminize me, but I loved the way this girl smelled, the way her hair curled, her skin smooth and white like a porcelain doll. It took no convincing to get me to spend as much time with her as possible, even if it meant learning to put on eyeliner. I preferred when she put it on me. Her soft hands would cup my face, her breath warm against my cheek, as she raised the pencil toward me. The soft tugs under my lashes as I stared up at the ceiling, listening to the soft click of her tongue as she applied it.

A few weeks before school started, she announced a first date with a boy, and in her bedroom—all hung with pictures of unicorns and horses—she declared that she needed kissing practice. So she asked me to pretend to be her boyfriend. I agreed. But we went on talking as usual, and we never kissed. I wondered if I was supposed to interrupt her, sweep her off her feet…? I thought she'd stop at some point and say, *okay, let's try it.* But she never did.

I never saw her not on the arm of a boy after that, and that was that.

'M FASCINATED BY Sandra's pencil skirt, which looks too perfectly fitted to allow her to sit down. But sit she does, at her desk in a small office down a back hallway of the museum. "I have various theories about who might have taken the peach."

I can't exactly let on that it doesn't matter to me who took it, but I play along. "Such as?"

"The plaque was also defaced at the time of the theft, which makes me think it was more likely anti-gay bigots than your typical art thief. But were they American or Chinese—or both? Were they acting alone or as propagandists? There are those who want to erase homosexuality from history, both in China and on the American right." The tapping of Sandra's heel betrays her agitation. "I redid the plaque and left the case boarded up to draw people's attention to it. More people have probably read it now than when the jade peach was sitting there."

I have to wonder why she's so invested, but I don't dare ask. "Me, I'm just amazed that there *are* things like that." My cheeks go hot as I realize how young I must sound. "My knowledge of gay history starts at Stonewall."

"Well, that's more than some people know." She pins me with another over-the-glasses glance. "Don't blame yourself for that. This is exactly why they're trying to suppress our knowledge and raise a generation in ignorance."

She doesn't look older than twenty-five, which means she could be as old as forty. Just yesterday I was mistaken for a junior high student, and it wasn't because of my backpack. Which reminds me I need to get a new ID, the kind that proves I'm twenty-one, but...that's complicated.

I try to steer us to the information I most need to know. "Can you tell me more about the peach itself? Do you have a photo of it?"

"Yes, of course." She shuffles through the stacks of folders on her desk. "If you know the history of the museum, you know the legality of some of our acquisitions has been questioned. And of course not all the pieces here were sourced ethically—"

"Does that mean you *do* or *don't* care how I go about getting the peach back?"

"Let's say Quan has never told me anything anyway, and I'd like to maintain that status quo. But." Her look hardens. "He knows we won't tolerate any kind of fakes or forgeries. I want you to know the same."

I nod. The thought hasn't even crossed my mind. "Understood." I ask a question that might sound irrelevant to the investigation, but of course it is not: "Do we have any idea the name of the sculptor and where he lived and worked?"

"Some attribute the work to a man named Chang Kuo-jung, who was a courtier about five hundred years ago." Sandra shrugs. "But the evidence is...heavily questioned by experts."

"The evidence?"

"Or lack thereof. There's a fairy tale, a myth really, about a jade peach being imbued with magical powers by a court magician, related to the story of the duke and his lover. The name of the magician matches the name of a government advisor in Xuanhua, and official records of his time serving the provincial court overlaps that of a man known to have provided several works of art to noble households in the city. If you believe the story, then Chang Kuo-Jung did the sculpting and this other fellow made the peach into a talisman that would tell a nobleman whether his love was true or not." She scoff-chuckles at that.

Well, Sandra Lim might not believe in magic, but I'm living proof that things aren't always what they seem. "You mean the peach could tell him whether his lover was faithful or not?"

"No, I mean *true love*. Supposedly he could give it as a gift, and if it was accepted by his true love, it would turn into a real peach. Some versions of the story say it would turn into the peach of immortality, so they could be together forever."

"Oh, really." I keep my face inscrutable.

"Anyway, either the noble never found true love, or it's just a romantic fairy tale, since last I saw it, the peach was still made of jade." This last comes with a final ironic chuckle and she hands me a glossy color print from the file folder.

It's of a green, white, and cream-colored piece of stone, delicately carved in the shape of a fruit, one leaf and a stem. The coloration makes it really look like a white peach that ripened on one side. "Fairy tales aside, I studied this piece for my masters thesis. I identified Chang Kuo-jung, and he would have done the carving some time in the year 4180."

Over five-hundred years ago. It sounds like a long time, but time and distance don't mean the same thing to me as they do other people.

I LEARNED A LOT of fairy tales from Jin Jin, but not the one about the bitten peach. Her storytelling started right on that very first night we met, when I was still so confused about so many things. I thought she was a bar hostess too, but she stayed upstairs while I was sent to make small talk in English with men who crossed over into Chinatown from the financial district or the big office towers by Government Center. I was told to expect big egos and big wallets, and that if I could get them to brag about how much they could drink, they would drink even more. At the slow point of the evening—when the dinner crowd had left, but before the late night crowd came in— everyone in the restaurant ate dinner. Cooks and busboys in stained whites emerged from the kitchen and joined waiters in ill-fitting bowties at a round table in the back. Some sat while others ate standing up, sitting as soon as another would leave, all of them digging into hand-sized bowls of rice with chopsticks and chattering on in a dialect I didn't recognize. From the looks and occasional words I could guess at, they were talking about me.

Too put off to vie for a seat, but not too timid to do something about it, I took a plate of greens and stir-fried fish with two bowls of rice and a handful of chopsticks, and before any of them could quite figure what comment to make, I marched upstairs to Jin Jin's room. She squealed with delight when I opened the door and hurried me to the small table there.

So, that was my first quiet meal with her, and the first time she told me a story. She told me a child's story because she hoped I would understand it, and eventually I did, and I told her one in return. I traded her "The Old Woman Who Lived In a Shoe" for the tale of seven brothers who all looked alike and fooled an evil emperor who thought that it was one man coming back again and again.

That's how trading stories became our ritual. Every night I went upstairs to find her watching the sunset, even in winter when it would fall in the afternoon. And we would sit at the mah jongg table (that's what the little table was, of course), her East, me South, sharing siao bao or yu choy or whatever and trading stories. These dinners were far better than any language class I'd taken, spending late nights in her room listening to fairy tales and rhymes meant for children's ears. She, too, learned English a word at a time, urging me on like an empress to an ambassador from a strange and faraway place.

Like the seven brothers, I returned again and again, looking the same, but I could feel I was changing.

RETURN TO THE museum the next day, after getting Sandra to promise to share her research notes with me.

I can't very well tell her I'm preparing for a five-hundred year old con job, but when I ask her to "indulge me" she doesn't say no. She brings all kinds of files: maps and drawings and printouts of computer translations.

For my part I try to project as much curiosity as possible. I can't predict which piece of information will come in handy. And it's all fascinating. "All this for an art history degree?"

"It's important to know the cultural context of the art," she says, her face placid, words ringing with the echo of old arguments.

"Does that mean...I don't know...that you know things like what sort of hats they wore?" I'm pretending it's an offhand question, but it would be useful for my disguise.

Her eyes go wide with delight. "As a matter of fact, I do!" She finds a stack of color photocopies of a long scroll of art and lays them out next to each other to connect several sections. "This is a court painting done for the lantern festival the year before Chang would have worked on the peach." She points out several figures, one seated on a platform above the others. "This is the regional governor, and these guys are his advisors." Next to them are some acrobats, leaping through hoops and balancing upon poles, while further over are some government ministers frolicking with firecrackers, their pleated robes in red, blue, or green looking almost like hoopskirted ballgowns as they hold up sticks with red sparks flying from their ends.

"And you know they're advisors from…the shape of their hats?"

"No. We know because their names and positions are listed." She smiles like it's a treat to meet someone who's interested in what she's been storing in her brain all this time, glancing up from the papers toward me. She flips forward a few sections of the scroll and shows me where a thick, green garden is inhabited by an orderly grid of bearded men, each holding a red lantern. "This one in the upper right is Chang Kuo-jung, and the one next to him is the supposed magician, Wang Gui."

"Wait, these are actual paintings of them?" All the men in the scroll look basically identical to me, their faces quite small, no bigger than a nickel, with tiny beards and tildes for eyebrows. "Did they really look like this?"

"I'm sure they were recognizable to their contemporaries, anyway. Have you seen the big paintings of the Hapsburgs in Vienna?"

"Um, no." I know even less European history than Chinese, but I have a feeling I'm about to learn some.

"You can tour the palace in Austria and it's wild. They would commission giant paintings—basically the size of an entire wall—for important events like royal marriages, and paint all the guests into the crowd.

There's one where you can easily pick out Mozart as a child. It totally looks like him." She laughs then and corrects herself slightly: "Or at least it resembles other portraits of him! The Hapsburgs were constantly marrying into other European royal families so you can pick out lots of princes and princesses, too. It just goes to show that the rich and powerful always want to immortalize themselves in art."

I squint at the image of the two men. Chang's hat is low and round, while Wang's is taller and rectangular. "Are all the guys wearing tall hats magicians?"

"No, but they're all advisors of some kind. As a *magician* his job was probably to interpret auguries and signs, and maybe predict the weather."

"So where was Xuanhua located?"

She dutifully drags out a map and pores over it. "There are some points in history where Xuanhau served as the capital, but in Chang Kuo-jung's day it was just one of the cities the imperial court occasionally visited." She slides her finger across the paper. "Beijing is right here and Xuanhau is just east of it. Nowadays the area is called Hebei, but at the time the prefecture would have been Zhili."

"Oh! I've been there," I say, before I can stop myself. "I...that, um, Five Dynasties bowl you have on display? That came from there." That one had been really easy to get. I arrived just before a huge imperial banquet. I and a hundred others were drafted into jobs in the kitchen, and I only had to stay long enough to abscond with one of the serving dishes that had been made for the occasion. Supposedly the conical shape was an innovation at the time.

"Yes, the kilns of Zhili were quite famous." Now she's studying me as if I'm a particularly intriguing painting, one that will start to make sense if she can just grasp the details. "You know, when Quan first told me about you, I assumed you were like him."

I am, but what does she mean by that?

She answers before I can ask. "The sort of person willing to smuggle out anything they think might be in danger of being seized or destroyed by the current government." But her brows draw together skeptically.

The thought that she doubts me skewers me to the spot.

"Now though, I don't know." She looks me up and down and my skin feels hot and cold. "I get the feeling you're more like a...a psychic or something."

Oh. In relief, I mimic her scoffing chuckle and deflect the subject from myself. "The current government wouldn't have wanted the peach displayed, you said?"

"It's why I worry that whoever took it might have destroyed it." A single worry line appears between her eyebrows.

I find myself wanting to reach out and smooth that line with my thumb. Instead I clench my hands. "Um, please try not to worry about that." I want to reassure her, but I'm not sure how. "All I can tell you is I believe the peach has a future as well as a past."

A little smile quirks the corner of her mouth. "All right. Hey, you know, if you're the one who brought us that Five Dynasties bowl..." She's examining me again, and I'm squirming out of reflex, but this regard feels warm, like the beckoning of an unexpectedly summery breeze.

She looks away for a moment. "Given that, I wonder if I might be able to take you out to dinner, on the department's tab."

I blink and panic. As usual, I'm in jeans and a flannel shirt. Starbucks is the only place I'm appropriately dressed for. "Um, tonight I have to—"

"No, no. Not tonight. You tell me when." She folds her hands at the edge of her suit jacket, suddenly demure and vulnerable.

My heart stutters. "Um, Friday." That would give me time to do some reconnaissance. "How about Friday?"

"Terrific!" She moves swiftly to her desk blotter to check the date. "Meet me here when the Museum closes? Since they're paying, we can go somewhere nice. I'll see where we can get a reservation."

"Oh, sure. Great. Yeah." This isn't the first time I wonder why certain women can reduce me to single syllables.

I leave as quickly as I can. I need to talk to Quan again, and then it'll be time for an excursion.

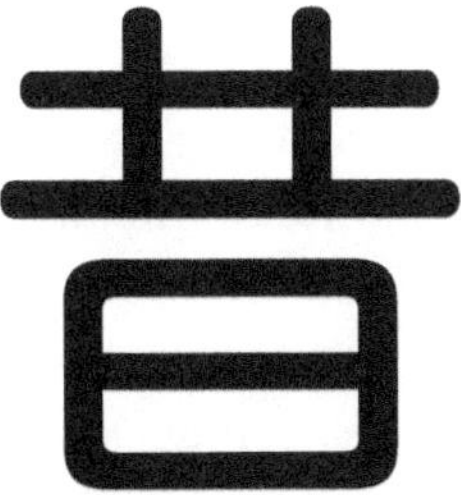

SOME OF THE stories Jin Jin told me sounded like they could have really happened, while others I thought she made up. I told her "The Three Billy Goats Gruff" in exchange for the story of a fishseller who begged the gods for a way to keep his fish fresh. They granted him a pill of immortality and as long as he kept it in his bucket, the fish would not die. His jealous rivals grew suspicious, though, and one day, while trying to hide the pill from them in his mouth, he swallowed it accidentally and so became immortal himself. I told her the story of Cinderella and she told me of a pair of young lovers who cheated the gods; the gods banished the woman to the moon, and her sad face peers down forever at her lonely partner on the earth. And when it came to people who became legends, like Robin Hood and King Arthur, I heard the stories of a princess who became a warrior, of a scholar who saved a city from demons, of the emperor's concubine who became immortal. In the days when concubines were buried alive in the emperor's tomb, her loyalty was so unwavering that it transformed her.

These stories were treasures to me. My mother had only read Mother Goose and Hans Christian Andersen to me, and never the stories of the seven lucky gods or of the dragon's daughter who could travel anywhere that the lucky red sky touched. Mom's one nod to "cultural enrichment" was taking me to the local diner that had been converted into a Chinese restaurant where they served dim sum every Sunday. They had the "Chinese Zodiac" printed on the placemats in bright red ink, but my mother—who resented being informed she was a pig—always said it was nonsense.

How wrong she was.

I STAND JUST INSIDE the screen door to the back alley at Quan's, waiting for him to get off the phone. He's prattling on in yet another dialect I don't know, sprinkling in English and a few others too quickly for my ears to adjust. When I travel, maybe because of who I am, I can usually catch on to the local dialect if I give it time—but I'll never catch up to Quan. He's had literal lifetimes to learn whatever he wants. How many languages does he speak, anyway? Instead of trying to pick out the words, I take in the tone of his voice—a hint of exasperation, some tension, impatience. Or maybe I'm projecting my own impatience.

Come on, Quan. Hurry up.

There's a beep as he presses a button on the phone, and he switches to English. Has he picked up another call? "Oh, are you there already? I'll be over in a few. Oh, yes. *Ciao.*" Italian, too?

He switches back to the other line, lets out a rapid flurry of words in Hokkien, this time, then hangs up and shoves the cordless phone into his pocket.

"You ready?" he asks me, as if he's been the one waiting for me for all this time.

I pat my pockets. "Think so. Check me over."

He pushes open the door to the alley and I step out so he can inspect me.

I have a small bit of money appropriate to the period, and I should be wearing the right shoes for our target era, the right jacket. I have my hair braided into a long queue down my back. I shrug my shoulders into a bit of a slouch and settle my underwear—the unseen part of the disguise. The one thing I can't fake is the necessary bit of bulge under the woven cloth of my loose pants. I scowl at him.

Quan chuckles. "If I didn't know better, I'd think it was magic, how you do that."

"Do what?" I pat at my clothes, concerned.

"Just become a man, like flipping a switch. If you put me in a dress, I still look like a fisherman wearing a dress."

"Oh, that." I shrug. "That's not magic, just acting." Compared to most of the fine feminine flowers of Chinese antiquity I've met in my travels? I can't even be measured on the same scale. I'm far more convincing as a young man, plus the disguise affords me necessary freedom of movement. "I've always been a tomboy."

"And I've always been a fisherman!" Quan laughs at his own joke. "Only now I fish for something else."

"If you don't see anything wrong, let me get going." I shoo him back into the shop so he won't get pulled along accidentally when I open the Gate. I know all too well how my power can fling a person halfway around the world in the blink of an eye. I'm a lot better at controlling it now, but it can still be wild.

The first time it went wrong was the night I found out
that one of the fairy tales was true. I had been working
at the restaurant maybe four months at that point, so
the outside air was autumn crisp as I came through the
kitchen entrance, into the perpetual steam and scent of fry
oil. I hurried up to Jin Jin's room as usual, only this time
the door was locked—from the outside.

I'd put my ear to the door, curious, perplexed.
Naïve.

I was supposed to be a decadent American, right?
Raised on uncensored television and subliminal sexual
advertising. But what did I really know? Nothing. I had
managed to never really think about why Jin Jin was
there at the restaurant. She wasn't a waitress or hostess as
I first assumed. She couldn't be a relative of Skinny's, no,
or she'd speak Canto, and not a sister of one of the cooks
who were mostly Fujianese. Not a boarder—if so, where
were her possessions? Her photos of home? I'd never
given a second thought to the Chinese men who often sat
and drank tea with Skinny Dou at the back table, and
sometimes went upstairs to play mah jongg.

It takes four to play mah jongg, but I'd never realized
it was a euphemism, until Skinny Dou pounded up the
stairs like a bull elephant to chase me away from that
room. He harangued me loudly, but I wasn't hearing his
words over my own thoughts: How can it be possible, I
asked myself, that a man in the 1990s can keep a whore
above his restaurant like a Chinese mail order "bride"
from the 1870s? I had thought a hundred years was a long
time, but now it seemed like no time at all. The past was
the present, and time and space that had once seemed vast
to me were suddenly small, and a place that had seemed
impossibly distant was suddenly close.

I'd reeled back from Skinny, suddenly dizzy—I couldn't
quite breathe. I fled. I clattered down the steps, not
looking behind me, listening to the heavy clang of utensils

against woks as I neared the kitchen, knowing that downstairs all would be as it had always been...

But it was not. The room was bigger, a live fish tank bubbled in one corner, and familiar-looking yet unknown waiters stared at me as if I had just fallen out of the sky.

I'd thought it had to be a trick of the architecture, and that I'd somehow come down the wrong set of stairs into the restaurant next door. I mean, what else could one reasonably think? Certainly not that I had ended up thousands of miles from where I had started. I rushed out to the street to find the air warm, the breeze heavy with humidity. Not comprehending, not knowing, I'd sat down with my back against the warm concrete of an alley wall and hid my face in my sleeves so no one could see me cry.

I have more finesse now. For one thing I've learned that stairwells are tricky and that doorways and arches work better. I like the back alley behind Quan's because the whole thing serves as a Gate. I do wonder what would happen if I tried using the big Chinatown Gate in Boston. Could I add a few thousand extra years to the jump? Except the streets there are never empty at dawn nor dusk.

But it's easy to go from one back alley stinking of fish blood to another. The shouts of shopkeepers echo off the walls as the alley multiplies into a thousand-thousand destinations. I step from standing between the buildings that I know to ones that I don't.

It's morning here. The alley opens onto a market that looks like it has probably been unchanged for centuries, rows of hawkers at their tables, selling things to eat and crockery and good luck charms. They are mostly men, but not entirely, calling out to each other and to their potential customers. Buildings—and dynasties—rise and fall, but somehow the people, like the writing, never stray far from what I expect. Is it something about their unchanging nature that gives rise to immortals in the first place?

The marketplace grows busier by the minute, as the cooks from the well-to-do households haggle for supplies. I listen, taking some time to catch the rhythm of this dialect, to understand the bend of the tones and the twists of the grammar. I'm the fisherman now, listening patiently, just waiting for a nibble on the line. Instinct has brought me to this particular place at this particular time.

There, I hear it—the name Chang Kuo-jung—spoken by someone to my right. But the knot of people pressing through is thick and whoever it was, I lose them in the throng. But at least I know I've come to the right time and place.

I eventually find the area where various day laborers hang about, hoping to be hired. They stand or sit in the shadow cast by the wall around a large temple. The ones still there by midmorning are either too old or too infirm for much of the work, but they are a good source of news, and like me they mostly don't speak the local dialect perfectly. They show me where I can exchange a copper for some duck eggs on rice, and tell me which drinking establishments are frequented by scholars and poets and which by soldiers.

I end up at one of these places where tea, liquor, and gossip all flow, but before I can enter, a man, his hair shot through with gray and loose down his back, stops me. "Hey boy." He has a conspicuous wet spot on his blue jacket. "Run an errand for me, eh?"

I put on my best callow scowl. "I'm already running an errand. Can you tell me where to find Chang Kuo-jung?"

He laughs knowingly and I wonder what it is he knows. He directs me to a different establishment, some distance away. I thank him and run off before he can engage me further, my shoes slapping the packed earth of the street.

The new place is on a street paved with stones. I can tell at a glance it is a different type of establishment altogether, frequented by a higher class of clientele, and, I suspect, serving vices other than mere alcohol.

The first floor is nominally a tea house, but the building's upper story is grand—with brass adorned shutters and a peaked roof that resembles one of the finer family manors. I know better than to try to enter through the front here. I go around the back where a cook, a thickset man with burly arms, is slaughtering a chicken on a round block of wood. He is heedless of the blood, but I wait until he is finished to try to speak.

But he speaks first. "What's your name."

"Wong," I lie. "I'm looking for Chang Kuo-jung."

The cook picks up a teapot and pours it over the bloodied chopping block. "Not here today." Something about his gaze tells me I'm not the first to come asking after Chang. "Were you sent to meet him here?"

"I...well..." I stammer.

My confusion comes across as something else. "It's all right, little brother," the cook says, plunging the chicken, feathers and all, into a pot. "No need to fear." Then he whistles.

A finely dressed man with his hair hidden under an elaborately folded, black silk hat appears on the landing above the outdoor kitchen. The two of them converse quickly in a dialect different from the one I've been hearing on the street. I might make out a phrase: "the attention of the great man."

The fancy man calls out to me. "Come inside."

He brings me through hallways of fine wood and up the stairs to a small room. Once there, he looks me over and I have the impression he is making sure I don't stink. He himself smells of cloves and frankincense, and the scent of burned wood clings to his silks.

Eventually, he gives me an approving nod. "Master Chang will be here for dinner. Afterward, he will see you." With that he slides closed the wooden-slatted door, and I am alone.

In the room is a low pallet made for a single occupant to sleep on, a small table, chair, and a chest set against the wall. I look into the chest, expecting to find bed linens, but inside are a set of brushes and stones, paper and smudge sticks. I guess this establishment caters to scholars who might have sudden and unquenchable needs for calligraphy? I sit on the pallet. I can only think of one reason why Chang Kuo-jung might have evening meetings with beardless young men like the one I appear to be. This is not going to work.

It's not something I can go through with even if I were willing to. After all, don't I lack something he expects?

A better strategy would be to find some way to get hired into his household. Perhaps next I should figure out where he lives.

I try the door and find it locked. I smile—mere walls cannot hold me, not with sunset arriving before Master Chang—but why do they feel the need to lock me in? Did many of their young men run off before their assignations? I really don't want to know.

WHEN I MADE it back after my first accidental jump—to Jin Jin, to the restaurant—Skinny Dou acted like nothing had happened. As far as he knew, I suppose, nothing did, other than me running away, upset. He didn't know I'd landed in Singapore, and honestly, it was still sinking in for me at that point. Everything in Boston Chinatown was exactly as it had been. The cooks, the stairs, the room, Jin Jin herself. What had changed was the light I now saw her through.

And I could not stomach the knowledge. I told her I was too ill to stay that evening, told Skinny I was too sick to work, and I left.

I didn't think I was going to return the next day.

But the next morning, I sat with my cornflakes, the TV on, in the kitchen I shared with three other students, and wondered what I was going to do with my life. What was I supposed to do? Work in an office and type on a computer?

Build automobiles? My mother wanted me to be a doctor like my father, but I was entirely certain now I was not going to be that. And what was a job for, anyway, just a way to have access to so many petty things needed to make up a modern life: ATM card, traffic reports, touch-tone phone service...?

I could not eat the cornflakes. I felt terribly homesick, but it was not my mother's home I thought of. The scent of the perfume in Jin Jin's hair and the sound of spatulas clanging on woks seemed to surround me, as if clinging to me from an early morning dream.

My worries felt foolish and small—yesterday I had gone down a stairway and emerged in a sun-filled city somewhere else in the world. Jin Jin might be Rapunzel, kept in her tower, but then I could be the knight. Even if we didn't fly halfway around the world, I had to at least help her escape from the restaurant.

Once I'd made up my mind to go back for her, nothing else seemed important. Midterm exams and cable TV and tire pressure gauges just didn't seem real anymore. I went back to the restaurant in the early afternoon, when I knew Skinny Dou would be sipping cheap baijiu with his cronies at one of the restaurants down the street.

She was asleep, wearing simple cotton and lying atop the daisy-print bedspread with her hair unbound. When she opened her eyes and saw me sitting there, she smiled.

I tried to find the words to either ask or explain, but what came out was, "I went far. But I came back."

She nodded eagerly. "You can take me back, then."

I thought she meant back to China. She did, but she also meant much more than that.

"You know, now," she added, and I thought she meant what she did for Skinny Dou.

"Yes, I know. I promise to take you back."

The moment I made that promise, it was like I unleashed her pent-up energy. All at once she was in motion, braiding her hair, crossing the room, unearthing a set of clothes from the bottom of the chest. She put on her finery and urged me into a jacket made of sturdy blue cloth, with wide pants and black shoes. We looked like we had stepped out of two different paintings, like I should be leading an ox while she should have a phoenix perched on her sleeve.

I hadn't necessarily meant that we should escape right at that moment, but why not?

I thought it would be easy. I thought we would just tiptoe out of there, and as soon as the sun began to set I would do what I had done to return from my accidental jaunt.

I hadn't counted on Skinny Dou coming back just then. I hadn't counted on having to pelt out of there at top speed, pulling Jin Jin along by the hand. I hadn't counted on Skinny grabbing a cleaver as he chased us through the kitchen, nor a couple of cooks following him, similarly armed, as he shouted, "Thief!"

As we ran, Jin Jin was urging me to go, *GO*, in every dialect she knew, but I couldn't stop to explain that I didn't think it would work. Sunset was hours away.

We sprinted around a corner, past the grocer with the roast ducks hanging in the window, and I tried to cut through a back lot to get us closer to the T station. But shouts arose ahead of us: the cooks from other restaurants were pouring out their back doors, too, trying to catch us. I'd seen this happen once before, when a couple of drunk guys had tried to dine and dash from a place on Beach Street. The word spread so fast they didn't get two blocks before they were surrounded and marched back to the place to pay up.

She urged me again. "Go, go!"

I had to try. I brought her to the back loading dock of the grocery and tried to picture it as a Gate. After all, it was sunset somewhere in the world, wasn't it? Something in my chest felt like it broke free and I sobbed as the doorways multiplied around us, spiraling. But it was all too fast, the wind whipping hard enough to make me shield my eyes, and even as I stepped through, Jin Jin screamed behind me. One moment she was flying beside me, and the next her hand was torn out of mine, as if a funhouse ride had flung us in opposite directions.

When I landed, I was in the Philippines, alone—my palm still damp where her hand had held mine, rapidly cooling as I stared in disbelief. I had lost her, and it felt like my heart and all my innards had been flung off into the void, too.

I needed to get her back. I needed to find her.

THE STEPS IN front of the museum seem vast, uncrossable. I hurry up them diagonally, angling toward the nearest door. As Quan likes to point out, how can a time-traveler be so chronically late? My tricks, unfortunately, can't speed up the subway or help me dress any faster. I discovered I own no appropriate clothes for accompanying a smart curator in a stylish skirt suit to a nice restaurant. The modern clothes I have are student wear—hoodies and jeans and graphic T-shirts.

When I dug through the drawers and my suitcase in my tenement room, I did find one silk shirt at least, made of a beautiful fabric patterned with dragons, black on black, but cut in a western style. Was it a shirt I had argued with my mother over? She'd wanted to make sure I packed a few "nice" outfits, no doubt imagining I'd need them to lunch with my advisor at the faculty club or when interviewing for internships or something, but she had vetoed some things in my wardrobe. We'd fought while I tried to get her to admit she thought they were "too Asian." She never did admit it, and I gave up trying to reason with her and hid the shirt inside a folded pair of jeans. Now I'm sure it's the same shirt, but it's not like it matters. It looks good on me.

In (clean) black jeans and a black leather jacket I at least look arty, if not upscale, and at hip New York City restaurants that's usually good enough.

Sandra's in her office, pecking away at the keyboard of a dusty-looking computer, seemingly unaware or at least unbothered that I'm late, and not at all bothered by what I'm wearing, either. She looks up at me in her doorway, smiles, puts her glasses back on and says only: "Ah, good."

That word, *good*, it sounds like a swallow, which I can't do because there's a sudden tightness in my throat.

She herself is in another stitch-perfect suit. She carefully unpins her employee name tag and sets it on her desk. "I've made us a reservation at a place in the Meat Packing District."

"Sounds great." I wonder for a moment if meat is actually packed there. The irony is not lost on me: I can navigate the back alleys of Shanghai, the night market of Kowloon, and the Forbidden City of Beijing, but I still don't know my way around the city where I supposedly live now.

We take the subway, which means a lot of time to stand and stare and think. The train's too noisy for conversation, and it's rush hour; everyone has their commuter faces on. Sandra stands with one hand wrapped around a silver pole. I'm a bit behind her, trying to figure out if that slight tang of citrus in the air is her shampoo or something else.

It's a business dinner, I tell myself. That's all. Isn't it?

And if she is interested in me? Then what? I fold my arms, crooking one elbow around the pole. I've never had a girlfriend (or boyfriend) yet. Just crushes. Soul-crushing crushes. But someone has to be the first, right? Life isn't entirely yearning for *everyone,* is it? Or is that just me.

WHEN JIN JIN and I were flung apart, the first
thing I did was search around near where I'd
landed. I made my way along the back doors of
laundries, bakeries, and bars, taking in the scent of soap
and fish and frying oil, and glimpses of the people...but no
Jin Jin. When I went around to the front, the shops were
all signed in Chinese, but the street name was Santiago. I
was in Manila.

The main street was gaudy with red lanterns and the
bright T-shirts of tourists. On one corner, two boys stole
a mango, one distracting the shopkeeper with a sudden
cry, the other hurrying past. Then they were both gone.
The shopkeeper looked at his neat stacks of roots and leafy
cabbage and fruit and frowned. Further down the row
from him, two old women argued at an open window with
a pharmacist, sending him up and down rows of hundreds
of tiny drawers in his shop in search of the cure for what
ailed them.

This could be happening anywhere, I thought, *on any street in
any Chinatown anywhere in the world.*

I found myself following two tipsy Taiwanese businessmen up the street, still in their business suits, their only concession to the weather taking off their neckties and undoing two buttons. One of them began to brag; my time as a bar hostess listening to drunks served me well. It took me a little before some words clicked, but eventually I realized one of them was bragging to the other about how many whores he could visit in a night.

The need to find Jin Jin surged along with my adrenaline.

"Here?" replied the other in horror, before he went on to disparage the locals for being below his standards.

To which the first one replied that there were one hundred percent Chinese-blooded girls to be had for a price.

I resolved to try to find her as quickly as possible.

WE COME UP out of the train onto a busy sidewalk. Sandra narrates like a tour guide. "This whole neighborhood changed almost overnight," she tells me. "In the eighties this was all warehouses and stuff, then the hardcore gay bars moved in, and now it's one of the hippest, most expensive areas."

"Oh really?" I say, because I feel like I have to say something. "Wait, so does that mean the *meat packing* was, um, you know..."

"A double entendre?" She laughs, light and carefree. "Just a punny coincidence, I think."

I'm blushing and trying not to. "Did you ever go to those places?"

"The hardcore gay bars? Well, they were a bit before my time, and they were really just for men." She gives me a glance. Yes, I'm that naïve and no, she's not that old. "The lesbian bars all moved to Park Slope years ago," she adds. "And now even Brooklyn's getting too pricey."

"Brooklyn?"

"Yeah, there was a real queer boom in Williamsburg." We're walking past a renovated warehouse that appears to house luxury condos on its upper floors, with a trendy restaurant on the ground floor obscured behind black one-way glass.

I forge ahead. "I haven't been to Brooklyn much. Is there a...bar there you like?"

"Restaurant's up here." Sandra gestures toward a building on the other side of the street. "There are a couple of places I like. If you're new in town, maybe some weekend I ought to show you around? We could take in a couple of galleries and do a dyke bar pub crawl."

I nearly trip as I step off the curb. That answers that question, doesn't it? I would never dare to say *dyke* so casually but she seems to use it in a proprietary rather than derogatory way. And, wait, is she asking me on a second date before the first one has even really begun? If it is, I'm agreeing to it before I can chicken out. "Um, I'd like that."

The restaurant is a chic Asian-fusion joint with a bar surrounded by illuminated glass and a menu of bewildering choices. A sushi bar that looks like it is built out of glowing, pink rock salt runs along one wall. People are in everything from torn jeans to Armani, so we fit right in. I let her order for both of us.

The evening goes by in a blur, partly thanks to the fancy sake we're drinking. I know my face must be scalding hot but that's fine: now when I blush no one can tell. At one point Sandra excuses herself to the ladies room, and when she returns, all I can think about is her freshly-lipsticked lips. We share dessert, a concoction made with green tea and Tibetan berries, and then we are out on the sidewalk again, both of our faces blazing.

"Would you like me to see you home?" Sandra asks. "Or have you had enough excitement for one night?"

Wow. I press my fingers against my feverish forehead. My grimy room in the tenement isn't somewhere to bring Sandra Lim.

"Thank you for dinner," I finally say. "Do you think, maybe, next week would be good? To go to Brooklyn together?"

Sandra laughs—the sake, or the glee, or the suddenness of it making her head tilt back and her hair swing. I like the look of her throat, tipped upward that way and wonder if she would like being kissed there. "Yes, sure. Friday or Saturday?"

"Saturday." Yes, Saturday. "And maybe I'll even have something to tell you about the peach by then." I'm about to try another jaunt to find Chang Kuo-jung. Tomorrow, in fact.

"All right. Leave a message at my office or on my cell phone and we'll rendezvous."

Sandra steps forward and presses a kiss silk-soft against my cheek. And then I'm watching her walk down into the subway, placing her heels carefully on each step, disappearing moment by moment.

Hours later, I notice the coral-pink imprint of Sandra's lipstick on my cheek. I get into bed without washing it off.

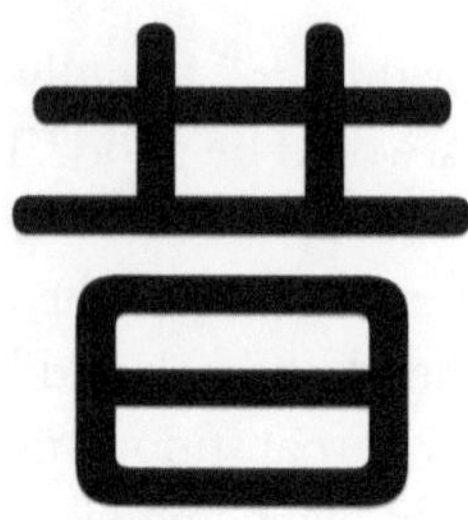

I WAS SO CLUELESS on those early attempts to find Jin Jin. At first I didn't even realize I was traveling in time as well as space. Thinking back, I have to wonder what year it was in Manila—possibly the 1970s? When I went back a second time, I dressed in my normal clothes instead of the outfit Jin Jin had put me in.

A restaurant with a shuttered upper story caught my eye and I went in. The dinner crowd was just starting to gather. I made a beeline for the bar against the back wall. The hostess was in a cotton blouse embroidered with flowers in a local style, but her upswept hair and red lipstick were familiar enough—she could have been one of my coworkers in a parallel life.

"Can I help you?" Her eyebrows went up when I sat down.

"What do you have for cold drinks?"

"Beer. And lychee on ice." She spoke English to me and I didn't question it.

I asked for the lychee on ice, not sure exactly what I would be getting. What came was a literal bowl of ice cubes with peeled lychee fruits nestled among them and a shot of something that might have been vodka. I pretended to sip it while I chatted with her about this and that and spooned juicy, cold lychee into my mouth.

"I worked as a bar hostess for a while," I finally told her. "At a dim sum palace stateside."

She laughed, covering her mouth as she did. "Are you looking for a job?"

"I'm actually looking for my…cousin," I lied. I had been going to say "friend" and I knew it would come out wrong. Jin Jin and I were closer than friends, even if I didn't have a word for what we were. I switched to Mandarin. "She does night work."

The hostess gave me a knowing nod and my heart leaped with excitement. And she repeated her question. "Are you looking for a job?"

"If I can be together with her, yes."

"Wait here." She disappeared into the back. When she returned, she beckoned me to follow her upstairs.

She led me through a parlor where several women sat, looking bored, while an electric fan attached in one corner of the ceiling blew hot air around. None of them were Jin Jin. We passed a room with a closed door, but the open transom above it let us hear every grunt and sigh from within.

"Wait here," she said again, indicating an unoccupied room. She closed the door as she left.

And I heard the door lock. That could not be a good sign for me. No, finding Jin Jin was not going to be that easy. I was going to need a better strategy, and probably a disguise. Escape was simple enough, but the experience redoubled my desperation to find her sooner rather than later.

But what does *soon* or *late* mean to someone like me?

CHANG KUO-JUNG IS an estimable enough personage that his home isn't difficult to find. Surrounded by a high-walled garden, it's not a palace, but a substantial household nonetheless with dozens of people in and out every day: servants, workmen, visitors. I spend a day or two at the teahouse down the street, watching the comings and goings and picking up gossip.

Some of the gossip is about me, of course. I speak very little to anyone, but they draw their own conclusions. I hear that I'm from one of the southern provinces, or maybe the west. I'm obviously from a family with too many sons, farmers most likely, and I am waiting until the next examinations are offered, or I failed the examination and am just being idle until my money runs out.

I would certainly fail that examination; my calligraphy is terrible. But maybe a lot of the boys from the countryside are like that. I practice writing characters in the packed earth with a stick while I sip tea and watch who goes in and out of the Chang compound's gate.

It's not like I can just slip into the building at sunset and steal the object. I don't even know if the peach has been sculpted yet, and if so, where would it be kept?

I might put the house into an uproar and force them to tighten security. I need to get a good look around inside, especially the workshop. Besides, I'm curious about this Chang. What sort of artist carves an object like the bitten peach—not just a tribute to true love, but to gay love?

When he comes down the street, I know him immediately. He's on foot, walking with another man. They are dressed in court finery, their jackets with one sleeve short and one sleeve long. In fact, the other must be the magician, because just like in the painting, he wears a rectangular hat, while Chang's is round. They talk animatedly, oblivious to those around them, making each other laugh. The cries of the bun seller and the entreaties of the monk selling charms seem not to reach them. As they converse, they pass through the gate into the Chang compound courtyard, ignoring the bows and obeisances of the servants until they pass out of my sight. What are they talking about, I wonder. Art? The weather? Court politics?

Soon after, a cart being pulled by a donkey comes to a stop in front of the gate, and the tired-looking cart driver uncovers a load of stone. For sculpting? Paving? It doesn't matter. It feels like my moment. I take my cap and leave my cup of tea behind.

The driver is happy to let me carry as many stones as I wish into the courtyard, where a servant directs me to pile them along one wall. Other laborers from the household join me, and in no time at all, the cart driver has said his goodbyes, whistled to his animal, and rattled away.

I turn to find the master of the house appraising first the collection of stones, and then me. Chang rolls a few coins in his hand but does not give them to me right away. Instead he asks, "Are you seeking work?"

"Yes, honored sir." I bow. I don't hold out my hand for the coins, though. "I have heard your artistry is unmatched, and I hope to see it with my own eyes."

He looks me over with fresh interest. "And what would a simple farmer's son know of artistry?"

"There is nothing simple about farming." I am making this up as I go along, of course. I latch onto something Quan said. "A single tea leaf seems like the simplest thing in the world, yet the mountain on which it grows, the amounts of sun and fog it receives in its life, and the time of year when it is plucked all add to the complexity of its flavor. This is how within a single sip a man may commune with the whole of nature."

Master Chang's mouth twitches—perhaps he is suppressing a smile. "It would appear you have a poet's soul."

"I am honored by your esteem." I bow and don't straighten while I make my plea: "Does the honored master require assistance?"

"As it so happens," he says, jingling the coins in his palm, "I do. The portents have spoken of the arrival of someone such as you. The work will be grueling. Your arms will ache. Your silence will be required for hours on end. But you will witness, as you called it, artistry. What is your name?"

I straighten. "Ping," I say, one of the names I use most because it's so common.

He tosses me a coin and I catch it by reflex. "Return at dawn tomorrow, Ping, and then we shall begin."

I bow and then watch him retreat into the house. This is a test, I realize. If I don't show up tomorrow, then it wasn't meant to be. If I do, though, then he'll see what I'm made of.

I'm made of sunset and dawnlight, but he doesn't know that.

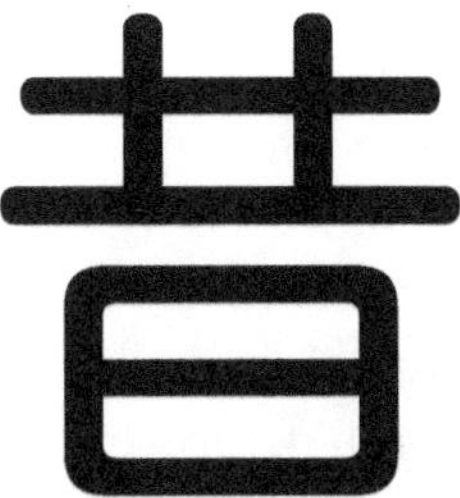

I RETURNED TO MANILA's Chinatown for another search looking very different from the way I had previously. By then I had been to Hong Kong, to San Francisco, to Shanghai, testing the limits of my abilities and concluding that I should circle back. In San Francisco I had the suit tailored, in a shop that I happened across by luck—of course, by luck—where I was far from the first customer to have undergone such a transformation.

Those picky Taiwanese businessmen had given me an idea: the best way to search for Jin Jin was to pose as a customer. Seeing myself in the mirror in the tailor shop, I found a kind of hardness on my face that was invisible when I was wearing women's clothes. I reached for the mirror by reflex, then touched my own cheek, fascinated by the difference. I remembered a fight with my mother before my senior prom. She'd wanted me to wear a frothy, frilly thing that looked like a wedding cake. I had wanted a piece of black velvet formalwear edged in red satin I had seen for sale in a Chinese catalog. It was one of the only times I heard her say out loud, *Don't you know we tried to raise you to be American for a reason?*

"We." As if she had my father's blessing. I had no way to know if she did or not. For my mother, happiness came from fitting in, from invisibility. I could never get her to understand that no matter how "American" I was, I could never be that invisible in white America. People always questioned if I belonged, with only their eyes if they were being polite, with their mouths if they weren't.

What will people say? she asked, if you wear a hideous Madame Wong dragon-lady dress? I had said if I had to go in traditional American formalwear, I'd wear a tuxedo. She shot down that suggestion, as well, of course.

In the end, I just didn't go at all.

But even when your face looks like everyone else's, it doesn't mean you're invisible. As I strutted up the main street of Manila Chinatown toward the brothels, I probably looked a little too slick, a little too Hong Kong maybe, compared to the regulars. But it suited me, it suited the act, when I marched into a place to inquire if they had any "pure" Chinese girls. It was just as stomach-turning as it sounds. When they said no, I could march back out in a huff.

The really vile part, actually, was when they would agree with me that Chinese girls were "cleaner" than the locals, or try to convince me of all the lascivious things that a local girl would do that other girls would not. My vocabulary and my knowledge of human sexuality expanded rapidly, but when I'd have to tell a girl no— sometimes very forcefully to stop her from trying to fondle the bits of me that weren't there—I'd usually end up crying in an alley by myself afterward.

I did not find Jin Jin on that trip, either. I needed help. I went to Quan.

This was before I knew him very well. In my experience, whenever a man asks me out to dinner, what he really wants is something else. Quan's the exception, but I didn't know that then. I'd found him when I went looking for an antiques dealer to get quick cash for my Manila trips, and he didn't even think it weird when I asked for the oldest bills in his stash. American money was the preferred currency for quasi-illegal transactions, and I had only just realized I could travel across eras as well as continents. I was also learning to trust the lucky red sky to carry me where I needed to go.

I wasn't surprised that it took me to New York City. I *was* surprised that it had taken me almost thirty years into the future. I had a couple of items with me from a pre-Mao jaunt; maybe they'd be more valuable the older they were? I had assumed an antiques dealer would be a crotchety old person, so I had been surprised to see he looked about thirty with the energy of a golden retriever. Nothing in the shop looked like it was from the 21st century: even the baseball cap on his head and the cash register seemed decidedly from the 20th.

I was thankful that he never pried into how I got what I brought beyond a casual "You must travel a lot." But from the second or third time I visited him, he had me fending off dinner invitations.

I soon gathered what intel I could from listening to the aunties gossip at the ice cream store and the bun shop down the street. Quan wasn't married, which only made me more suspicious of him pressing me to go eat with him. He told me he inherited the store from his father, but the aunties never mentioned an elder. He fancied himself a historian, and I enjoyed listening to his stories, even though he never talked about himself. That was only fair, since I never talked about myself, either. Something didn't add up, and I found myself getting more and more curious.

I didn't give in to his invitations, though, until I needed more from him than he needed from me.

JADE, IT TURNS out, is not carved or chiseled as I imagined it would be. No, it must be ground down painstakingly like glass.

Master Chang does his work first with grinding saws of ever smaller sizes run on a foot-treadle, then with finer and finer grinding pastes.

On the first day, he shows me that the roughest paste is yellowish in color, the finer one reddish, the next finest black, and the finest of all quite red. It isn't until I see the whole stones from which the pastes are made that I finally understand they are ground semi-precious stones themselves: quartz, garnets, almandines, and rubies. Whole treasures unto themselves being ground to dust in service of this art.

My first task as his assistant is to destroy one of these, and I hold the crushing stone in my hand, trying to move past my surprise, but I'm paralyzed by my realization. No wonder jade sculpture carries such immense value. Would a farmer's son even know that one stone was worth more than another?

"Like this," Chang says, his arms encircling me, his front pressed against my back, as he shows me how to position the crushing stone. Together our hands reduce a garnet to dust and once I have gotten past my awe, I can't help but grin. He leaves me to it while he turns his attention to polishing a recently finished piece, a small statue of a crouching rabbit, its ears flat along its back.

Later, as he begins work on a new piece, my task is to hold a reflective panel so that the light will be evenly bright on all sides of the stone. I have been admonished not to move, or even breathe too hard, so that the light remains steady. The stone he has chosen is about the size of a mango and incorporates several colors. Could it be the peach?

"Honored sir," I say, to distract myself from the burning sensation in the muscles of my arms, "what will it be when you are finished?"

He does not smile, but his face radiates a kind of wounded serenity anyway as he answers: "It will be a token of love."

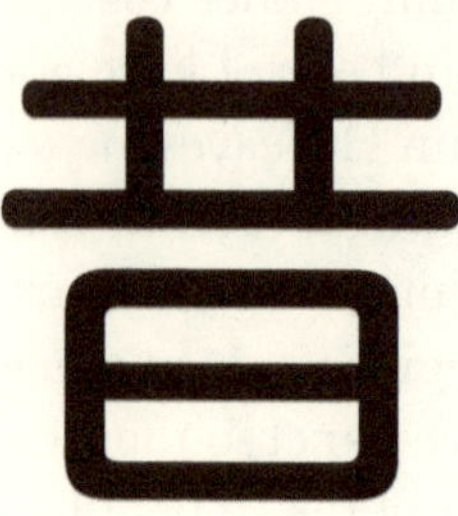

I COULD SEE QUAN through the window, a loupe to his eye as he examined some treasure or another under the circle of light on the countertop. The rest of the place was dark, but I knocked on the glass and he hurried over to let me in.

"Mei-mei! I was wondering how long it would be before I saw you again. Been traveling?"

"Yeah, Manila again," I told him, seeing no reason to hide it, not when now I was going to enlist his help. How much was I going to have to tell him, I wondered, and would he even believe me?

"Bring me anything good?"

"This time?" I held up my empty hands. "Only...a good story, I think."

His eyebrows went all the way up. "What kind of story...?"

"A fairy tale, maybe?" I cleared my throat. "How about I tell you over dinner?"

His delight was instantaneous. "Of course, of course! How about Lu Bo Lang? Still the best dumplings in town. And they do Peking Duck on demand."

I didn't actually care what we ate, but I knew the place he meant. "Not some place where we have to share tables."

"Ohhh." He nodded knowingly and I worried he misconstrued my request for some privacy. "Hunan House, then."

"I don't want people to hear what we're saying."

"Hunan House will be perfect, then. It's so noisy in there no one will hear us."

I wasn't sure how that could be true, but I followed him. At the bottom of the stairs leading down into the restaurant, he spoke to someone, and they seated us next to the kitchen doors.

After we sat, he seemed anxious, and that made me nervous, like I'd really messed this up and was walking straight into a marriage proposal or something which would ruin our friendship. His hands shook a little as he poured us both jasmine tea, and we sat there, each with a cup under our nose, not saying anything. I still had no taste for tea but it did smell nice. Above the table was a kind of garish painting of one of the folk tales Jin Jin had told me, the one about the immortal fishseller.

"You promised me a story," he finally said, looking up at the painting. "Do you know this one?"

"In fact, I do." I set down my cup, suddenly overwhelmed with longing for how Jin Jin used to brush my hair and trade stories with me. "It's about how the seven lucky gods gave an immortality pill to a fish seller, but he swallowed it by accident, thus becoming immortal himself."

Quan tried to keep from laughing, but he couldn't hold it in. "Who said it was an accident?"

Thinking he was just spitballing, I played along. "Sure. What would happen to him then? If that's not the end of the story, then it's more like a beginning, right?"

"Oh, he traveled the world, went to every continent to taste their fruits and their wine, and eventually found his mortality slipping back, bit by bit. Until he went home, and then the seven lucky gods smiled on him again." His smile was as wide as the whole fish the waiter put down between us, fragrant with ginger and scallions.

I stared at him, still not comprehending. "Cute."

He dug into the fish expertly with the serving spoon, right at the spine, and slipped a generous chunk onto my plate while the waiter set down two small bowls domed with rice. "Okay, how about another one. Do you know the one about the Dragon's Daughter?"

My hands froze with my chopsticks halfway to my mouth. "I...might."

"Mei." He sighed. "I know who you are."

I was so annoyed. "Like hell you do." Here I'd been debating for so long about whether to tell him or not, and he already knew.

He could not keep his glee trapped behind his teeth. "I know you're an immortal because I'm one, too."

And then it clicked. "You're the fishseller!"

He flourished his chopsticks like an opera star's fan. "One and the same! Though I'm often mistaken for Wong Fei Hung. I suspected you were the Dragon's Daughter the moment you walked into my shop."

Although he looked exactly the same as he had the moment before, my mind was rearranging everything I knew about him. "So that story you told me about inheriting the store from your father was untrue." I tried to wrap my head around it. "Your life must be kind of complicated?"

"Eh, sometimes. Mostly I have learned to lead a simple life because I enjoy it."

"But don't people get suspicious? I always wondered why you were single."

"Bah. So do all the aunties who work at the bubble tea shop," he joked, but a little bit of a lonely note rang in his voice. "It's true, a relationship could be very complicated. I try not to get attached. Am I the first other immortal you've met?"

"Yes!" I said, then immediately reversed myself. "No! There's...there's one other. But I lost her. I'm trying to find her."

"Oh, who?"

"Jin Jin," I said, but he didn't know that name. But now that I knew all the stories she had told me were true, it all seemed so clear. "The Emperor's Concubine."

His mouth opened in a silent *oh*. "Yes. She Who Pines."

"You've met her?"

He shook his head. "I'm not her type. I have heard tell of her, but not in a long time."

"She's waiting for me," I insisted, banging my fist on the table like I had something to prove. "You have to help me find her. How do you know about other immortals, anyway? How did you know who I was?"

He pushed a rice bowl at me. "Eat before it gets cold, and let me try to answer one question at a time. When you first came in, all I knew was that you were some kind of immortal. I wasn't sure what kind."

"There are different kinds?" I blurted, before retreating behind my rice bowl. "Sorry. One question at a time. Right."

"Only you would be able to bring me things like you did. But here's how you tell who's immortal. Put your hands in your lap. Take a deep breath. Let it out. Now soften your eyes."

I put my hands in my lap but I had to ask, "What do you mean, soften my eyes?"

"I mean...do the opposite of staring hard at things."

I pretended to know what he meant just to humor him, but as I sat there, I did manage to defocus my eyes, and I saw the shift. The world around us became as flat and insubstantial as the painting of the folk tale on the wall, the voices of the people as muffled as a radio in an apartment next door, but Quan remained solid and bright. I blinked, startled, and the sound and color of the restaurant around us snapped back to reality. "Whoa."

"Now tell me how you lost her." He urged me to eat again, this time just with gestures.

So in between bites of red snapper and rice and mustard greens with garlic, I told him the whole saga of how we met at the restaurant in Boston, in the 1990s, when I was still a freshman in college.

"And how long ago was that for you?" he asked.

It felt like it had been years, but actually, "Since losing her? I guess just..a few months."

I realized it hadn't even been a year since my discovery that I could fly from place to place. I told him about that, of course, and everything right through the part where we were chased through the streets by cleaver-wielding cooks and how I let go of her hand while the Gate was open. I told him she could be almost anywhere.

By the end of my story, his face had turned serious and solemn, reflecting in his teacup like the lonely moon. "Hm. She might even be here in New York."

My heart leapt. "You think so?"

"I will ask around."

O N SATURDAY AFTERNOON, Sandra takes me through a bunch of funky art galleries in Brooklyn. Weekend-Sandra seems younger, maybe because she's not in work mode, not just that she's wearing fashionably cut jeans and a vaguely Indian print shirt of blue and orange. The first gallery on the agenda has huge oil paintings of figures that make her shirt seem muted. To my uneducated eye, everything on these canvases looks kind of like Picasso, so I feel vindicated when the manifesto on the wall acknowledges Picasso's influence. It also declares the artist's use of color to be "feminist" which I can't really see, but maybe I just have to believe it's there?

Sandra says "Hmm" as she reads it and then moves on to the framed works. I can't say I'm impressed until I notice the display of jewelry on a table near the back. A curator/saleswoman is explaining to another woman that each pendant is a miniature recreation of one of the paintings, made by the artist herself. For some reason I find this far more impressive and intriguing.

As we're walking from there to the next gallery, I ask Sandra if she saw the necklaces.

"Interesting, right? Clever, too, for so many reasons."

The sun is high in the sky and sweat is starting to stick my shirt to my back under my leather jacket. "Why clever?"

"For one, the artist is offering something at a lower price point that people can buy if they want to be supportive, but can't shell out a few thousand for a big canvas. Some people really want to feel like they have ownership over a unique artistic creation, so the pendants are a really new and different way to confer that feeling other than hanging the art on the wall. On top of that, each piece becomes a kind of advertisement for the art." She sweeps her hair into a loose bun and clips it, fanning her neck with her hand. "Maybe *advertisement* isn't the right word. It becomes a conversation starter, anyway. And jewelry like that is mostly going to be worn by women and talked about with other women. Just a great move. My mother would love that sort of thing—"

She freezes suddenly, her eyes darting back like something might be in pursuit.

"Everything okay?"

She weighs something in her mind, then asks, "Do you mind if we go back? Mother's Day is coming up..."

We return to the gallery and she picks out a necklace and then waits while the gallery clerk painstakingly packs it with a box and tape and mylar sleeve. "My mother was very skeptical of me studying art," she tells me while we wait. "She especially wasn't sure about me studying ancient Chinese art. But now that I work for a prestigious institution that her friends have heard of, now suddenly it's okay to brag about me a little bit. Ha. So a little reminder conversation piece..." She accepts the paper bag across the counter and hands over her credit card.

"Mine didn't want me learning Chinese," I say. "Like it might give me an accent and then I wouldn't fit in."

"Right? My parents argued about it. They wanted to be assimilationist but my mother also had friends who sent their kids to Mandarin lessons once a week. So I did that until I was about thirteen and got too busy with school." She holds in a small laugh. "When we argued about me specializing in Chinese art, I was a bit of a little shit about it, too. 'But Mom, why did you have me go to Chinese classes all those years if I'm never going to use it?' That sort of thing." She tucks her wallet and the necklace into her purse. "Well. I hope she likes it."

She doesn't ask if my mother might like a necklace, too, but I can feel her curiosity looming like summer humidity. *I haven't spoken to my mother since I left college...* I think but do not say. I settle for, "I'm sure she will."

I follow her into the next gallery, a small bell tinkling on the glass door as we enter. The window is covered in dark-tinted plastic, making it cool and cave-like inside. The space is long and narrow, with glass cases placed under lights spread along the walls, an unlit path snaking between them.

In each case sits a sculpture made of melted, fused glass. Some reflect the light from within, while others have flecks of reflective foil on the surface. Most of them are abstract, but they have a kind of suggestive or sensual curve to them. I lean close to Sandra and whisper, "You know, the use of the S-shape is *feminist*," and Sandra snorts, covering her mouth with her hand.

In the next case, though, is something that makes us both stare. It's a glass representation of a peach. *That* peach?

The curator, a white woman in a long cardigan and long red braids, notices us lingering over it and joins us. "The artist is drawing on her heritage for this piece," she drawls, "as it is based on a historical Chinese account and is not only a symbol of prosperity, but a statement about same-sex marriage. I can't help but notice you two ladies are both of an Asian extraction. Are you looking for a statement piece? This one is ideal for a small apartment."

This time it's me who snorts and has to cover my mouth. Sandra asks if the woman has a card or catalog of the artist and is handed a brochure, then hustles me out onto the street.

She's laughing as we head toward the train station. "Nothing more awkward than a hard sell!" She puts a hand on my waist as we wait for the walk signal, though. "I guess we do look a bit like a couple."

"Well, this is a date, isn't it?" I try to say it lightly, like it's a joke, but to my own ears I just sound high strung.

"I'm under the impression it is," she agrees. "Let's stop and get a drink. I'm parched."

Yes, I'm quite thirsty.

H AVING SURVIVED A day of work with the master jade carver, I am given a place to sleep at Master Chang's home with the other servants. It's in an outbuilding attached to the main house by a wooden covered walkway, allowing the staff to come and go without tracking in mud or getting drenched by the heavy summer rains. The gray-haired man who tends the compound's fires and lanterns tells me that, unlike some artisans whose workshops bustle with journeymen and apprentices, Master Chang prefers to work alone or with just one helper, like me. "Ours is not one of those like Master Puo's, where they spit out a hundred vases at a time like a bakery," he says with derision. "Master Chang works only when his energy is high and his lungs are clear."

"Did you say *lungs*? You mean breath?"

"I do mean breath, little brother," he tells me. "Be sure to wear the cloth he gives you to keep the dust out."

I bow to show I will. "What happened to the helper before me?"

The old man chuckles. "Do not be so apprehensive! He moved on to better paying work once he was old enough to start thinking about a wife. You're far too young for that!"

I heartily agree. This explains why Master Chang so easily accepted my story that I may have to be gone from time to time to help an uncle who is a fishseller by the lake. (The best lies have a grain of truth.)

The next morning I share a meal with the other laborers before I am summoned to the workshop. Today, as Master Chang works the treadle, I am tasked with refilling the container of water above the saw. Water flows constantly as the jade is ground. Four buckets are aligned to one side, and when he begins work, the open reservoir above is nearly full. Once it gets down to a certain level, I must climb up with a bucket and carefully pour water in, and then do it a second time. The quantity is enough to give me time to take the two empty buckets to the well, fill them up, and return in time to refill the chamber once again.

Each time I return, the piece of jade has been worn down a bit more. The color being revealed is beginning to look familiar, a blush of gold-pink on one side, and green on the other. It still looks more like a mango than a peach, but I know eventually it will have a stem and leaf as well. I am mesmerized watching the outermost layer be gradually stripped away by the trickling water and the grinding paste and the gentle rocking of Master Chang's foot on the treadle, and at least twice he admonishes me to keep an eye on the water level. But I never let it get much below halfway empty.

By the time we cease work for the afternoon and Master Chang goes off to visit with friends at a teahouse, I am worn out, but exhilarated at the same time. I eat hungrily with the other servants and listen to the gossip around the house. This is how I learn that Master Chang has no wife. "The fortune tellers always say it would be inauspicious to seek a marriage with him," one of the housekeepers says to another, "even though he has plenty of money and a wife would be welcome here!"

The other one scolds back. "Ayah, we don't need the word of the fortune tellers. Master Chang has the favor of the governor and all his ministers, and that is all the good fortune he needs."

"Isn't our master good friends with the magician, Wang Gui?" I ask, just to see what they will say.

"Oh, that one!" She shivers as if the thought of him scares her a little, but her smile is broad. "At new year, he predicted health and good luck to all in the household, and when the spring fevers came, though it struck many in the city, we were spared."

I remember Master Chang saying he had a prediction that I would arrive, too. Was it Wang Gui who foresaw me coming or another fortune teller? I will have to remember to ask Quan what he thinks, next time I see him.

After the women have left, the lamplighter points in the direction they went with his chin. "Silly birds they are, chirping on about why the Master has no wife, when everyone in town knows of our Master's eccentricities."

My heart sinks, remembering that fancy teahouse where they locked me in a room, and I dare not speak, but I ask with my eyebrows.

He seems surprised. "You don't know? He spends many an evening at a place in town, where they find only the most beautiful boys for him." He lowers his voice conspiratorially. "And then he takes them to a private room."

"And then?" I squeak.

"And then he *draws* them."

I think at first I've misheard or misunderstood. "Draws them?"

"Yes, portraits in brush and ink. But that's not all."

Now the other shoe drops, I think. "No?"

"No." He makes a clucking noise with his tongue that surely means that he is about to reveal the most scandalous behavior of all. "Then he burns them."

"The boys?" I ask in horror.

"No! No no no." He shakes his head. "The *portraits*."

"And that's all? Nothing else?"

"Nothing else. Our Master is too pure of soul. But this is why no woman will marry him."

"Because he's too pure…?"

"Because he is so devoted to his art," the lamplighter explains patiently. "Master Chang is a good man and we are honored to serve him, but a wife would not feel so."

I decide I cannot get into a debate about gender roles, so I merely bow in assent.

THE BAR SANDRA takes me to is small and dim except for the rainbow flag in the window and the neon along the glass shelves of liquor. It doesn't look much different from other American bars I've seen, though admittedly I haven't been in many. I have the slight problem that I don't have the proper ID. If I go back to the year I turn 21, I suppose I can get the license I need... but it'll be expired when I return. I'll have to then jump to the renewal year...? I suppose it will be worth it to put up with the comments about how Asians don't look our age. Maybe asking Quan to get me a fake ID would be easier. He must've figured this out by now, right?

But they don't bother to ask Sandra for ID and she orders two beers and pays for them while I carry the bottles, cold-sweating, over to a table where we can watch two women playing pool.

There's a large painting hanging on the brick wall behind us that looks kind of Rennaisance-y to me, of some Greek or Roman goddess, her flowing hair doing nothing really to hide her nudity, which I suppose is the point. "Is it a real painting?" I ask, as we sit.

Sandra glances behind her and then at me. "It's not your imagination," she quips. Before I can feel at all stung by that, though, she goes on. "It's a reproduction, but a pretty old one in and of itself. I wonder if a woman painted it or a man?"

Or someone who was neither. "Does it matter?"

"Well, the original was a man." She doesn't bother to tell me who, though. "Throughout Western art history you find all these horny guys trying to come up with reasons to paint nudes, and no matter how repressive the mores of their society, there was always some way. Like, 'oh, this isn't a nude *per se*, it's the Virgin Mary offering her milk to the baby Jesus,' and somehow that was okay and not blasphemous? Or, hey, it's okay because these are Greek goddesses and nymphs and they were classically painted that way, and if it was good enough for the Greeks it should be good enough for us."

I take a gulp of my beer and it leaves my lips numb and wet.

She lets her hair free of the bun and it brushes her shoulders as she shakes it out. "I've heard it said that the creative impulse on the part of an artist—whether they are a painter, writer, sculptor, musical composer—lies very close to the erotic impulse. So it's no surprise that the great painters painted nudes up the wazoo." She glances back again. "And the art market has always been mostly men as well, whether private collectors and rich speculators like today, or patrons in the Renaissance, or those in charge of commissions for institutions like churches or governments."

"You're saying it's horny men all the way down."

I'm watching the couple playing pool. One of them is in a sundress, the other in jeans and a T-shirt.

"Men want to own beauty, whether it's in the form of art or a woman—or art of a woman. They want to own it and control it. In the art world, that comes easily if you have the money." She takes a sip of her beer, her eyes also on the couple at the pool table now. "It's why I can't have relationships with men."

I feel like I'm supposed to reach out and grab her hand now, or something. Instead, I ask, "And women don't want to own beauty?"

She blushes, or maybe that's just the alcohol making her skin flush like mine. "I shouldn't generalize so widely, I know. But it never works out for me with men. They always want to treat me like a Ming vase, like a pretty, exotic prize."

But you are pretty, I want to tell her.

As if she hears my thought, she says, "I've always been femme."

And I never have, I realize. I could put it on like a costume—for a prom, or to hostess at the bar—but that's all it was. A costume. But so was the tailored suit I wore to Manila. Just as much as the poor scholar's robe and hat I wear to Master Chang's. Or the clothes I'm wearing now.

I jump a little at the clack of the pool balls: the woman in the jeans has struck some kind of definitive shot, and she raises her arms in triumph. Her partner kisses her on the cheek, and then finds herself bent back against the pool table, their knees interleaved.

Sandra then asks, "What about you?" unaware that inside I'm asking myself that same question, but far less casually.

The butch has literally slid her hand inside the femme's dress and it's somehow never occurred to me before that maybe a dress allowing easier access than pants is a tool of the patriarchy, except when it's not.

This is when I'm supposed to tell her about myself. About my exes or my preferences or my labels for myself. About my relationship with my mother or lack thereof. About who I am. That's what's supposed to come next.

"I have to go," I say, standing up as if I just realized I left the stove on. "I—"

I pull her hand off the beer bottle and kiss it, resisting the urge to suckle the condensation from the soft patch between her thumb and palm, and then I do what I am good at, which is run away.

REMEMBER WHEN QUAN had said there was more than one kind of immortal? I'd held my tongue at the time, but he had to tell me eventually. He poured me tea in the cramped back of the shop, where we sat on folding stools with a brown clay teapot between us. The tea was much darker than usual; it tasted like roses, definitely roses, which meant it was more like drinking an old lady's perfume than the usual lawn mulch. I refrained from teasing him about it, though, because what we were discussing was too serious.

"No leads in New York," he told me, "at least not in the present day."

I slumped in defeat, but also partly in relief. If he'd found her there, she would have been waiting over twenty years for me to show up. "What am I doing in the twenty-first century anyway?"

"Mei." He reached up and touched his own breastbone with one finger, like he was pointing to a spot on a map. "You came forward to find me, remember?"

"But why? Why couldn't I have just come to you in 1992? You were here, right?"

He nodded. "But you didn't. Mei, I want you to take a deep breath."

Here we go again, I thought. "Yes, sifu," I said, in the most sarcastic impression of a kung fu student I could muster.

"Just think. How does your power work?"

"Well, I open infinite gateways...and then...I just pick one."

"And is what you choose truly random?"

"No. I mean, it doesn't seem to be. I don't know exactly how I choose, but I get a sense, I guess. An intuition."

He nodded again. "There is not just one tale about the Dragon's Daughter; there are many. Mei, when you really use your power, you go where needed. Either where you need to, or where you're needed by someone else."

I took a sip of the tea, waiting for him to say more, but he stopped there. "Are you saying she doesn't need me?"

Quan gave me a long-suffering look. "Do you feel like she doesn't need you?"

"No! I can feel her yearning." Or maybe I was projecting my own yearning, but I didn't say that. "Yearning," I repeated. It tugged on my proverbial heartstrings like the plucking on a gujin, reverberating through time and space.

When Quan poured me fresh tea, my cup tinkled like a tiny bell. "You know the story, her story, right?"

"Of course. She's the Emperor's Concubine," I said, annoyed that he was bringing it up. Some emperors had their wives and concubines buried alive so they could serve them in the afterlife. Others had them drink poison. But I guess that hadn't deterred her. "The woman so loyal that the gods granted her immortality, right?"

He shook his head. "No god came down and gave her a pill, Mei. She's not like me. She transcended her individuality. A different kind of immortal."

I took a sip of the perfumey tea, knowing if I just kept quiet he'd explain.

"I'm the god-granted kind who's lived one long life. You're the kind that is reborn again and again. She's... something else."

"What then?"

"She's the embodiment of an ideal. An archetype. The yin that the power that is yang demands as balance."

"So?"

"So maybe she could love an Empress, too. She's still an embodiment of the power behind the throne, and her loyalty to the throne is what makes her what she is. She is...*perfect*. But that means she can never change."

"I know that!" I don't know why a tear decided to roll down my face right then. "I know she wants some Emperor and not me. I promised her I'd bring her back. I just want to keep my promise, is all."

He looked into his tea and set it down and fussed with pouring some more so he could ignore the fact that I was wiping my cheeks on the sleeves of my sweatshirt.

He was still looking into his teacup when he said, "I wasn't sure you could say that out loud."

Well, neither was I, until I'd done it.

"Mei," Quan said, "I think I know where you'll find her. Because it's the one place you've been avoiding."

The strings of the gujin on my heart thrummed uncomfortably.

"You never went back to Boston to look, did you?"

Shit. "No. I was afraid to."

"Was. Does that mean you're not afraid now?"

No, it didn't mean that at all, but— "I can bring you with me!" I warmed to the idea instantly. "You can go in and check if she's there!"

"Me?" He almost spilled his tea.

"Yes, you! They won't know you so they won't be suspicious. You can go to the bar and order the house specialty. What, are you too busy with your spring cleaning?" I looked around the crammed storeroom. "I'll bring you right back. Besides, didn't you just say it was Fate that we met?"

"I never used the word Fate."

"You know what I mean. I found you for a reason. This is that reason." My conviction was so strong it left no room for argument.

The only preparation we made for the trip was Quan replaced all the newer bills in his wallet with old ones.

And then we stepped out into the sunset.

"**P**ING. HURRY UP."

A housekeeper's voice wakes me and I shake myself. Dawn already? My arms still ache from yesterday and the days before that. Master Chang has been working long hours on the peach every day. That has meant long hours of me standing perfectly still, not speaking. Long hours for thinking about what I should say to Sandra the next time I see her. *Sorry I ran off, but I think I like you too much…?*

I have come to no conclusions. When Master Chang asks me what I'm thinking about, I tell him I'm ruminating on the nature of love, which is basically true.

This morning I hurry through my own preparations and then into the workshop where the artist is already seated, but not at the grinding treadle. He is working on a piece of paper lying flat on the worktable. I look over his shoulder and see it is a painting of a peach, as gold and rosy as daybreak and as full as the moon.

"I didn't know you could paint also," I say, because I'm still too sleepy not to be stupid. *Of course* he can paint.

He smiles at my comment. "I prize the naivete of your eyes. What do you think?"

"It looks good enough to eat."

That seems to satisfy him. He sets down his brush and takes up another, this one finer, and dips it into the stone dish that holds the black ink.

His hand is too stylized for me to be able to read all the words, but I gather it's about the peach. And maybe love. "Is that a poem? About the peach?"

"Just so." Chang chuckles at my frown of effort. "It compares the wonder and sweetness of the growing fruit with the budding of attraction and the growth of friendship and esteem, for what is the purpose of such a fruit in life if not to be bitten?"

"And all the sweeter for being shared?" I ask.

He clucks his tongue, as if that would be going too far, though I can't tell if it's because it's too obvious or if it's violating some cultural norm. "There is a good deal of poetry you had best learn. Perhaps I shall teach you to read properly, after this is done. Which will be soon. Maybe even today." He gestures toward the small lump sitting on the grinding wheel under a piece of silk, as if the stone were still sleeping.

My heart skips a beat. Nearly done! "Is a rich nobleman awaiting it?"

"You could say that." Master Chang sounds amused. He motions to me and I help him remove his beautiful silk outer robe. He replaces it with one as plain as mine before he sits at the grinding wheel. "I am awaiting its completion, myself. It is to be a gift."

"Ah." I bow slightly.

He bares the unfinished peach and contemplates it. "Once I have perfected the form, there is still one more step to be done, for which I will need the help of someone else."

"Someone besides me?"

Chang chuckles again. "Yes, Ping, though you do fine work." He gestures for me to lift the reflecting board and brighten his work surface. "I shall need the help of my oldest friend, Wang Gui." His voice has a kind of melancholy in it, as if he hasn't seen Master Wang in years.

"You sound as if he's very far away," I say.

My stupidity makes him laugh. "No, no, although one might say that by living inside the walls of the administrative district, he lives in another world. I will leave this piece with him for a time so he will be able to imbue it with charms."

"Why does it need charms?"

"Oh, to make it lucky," he says airily, as he lets the square of silk fall, his answer far too insubstantial to be the truth.

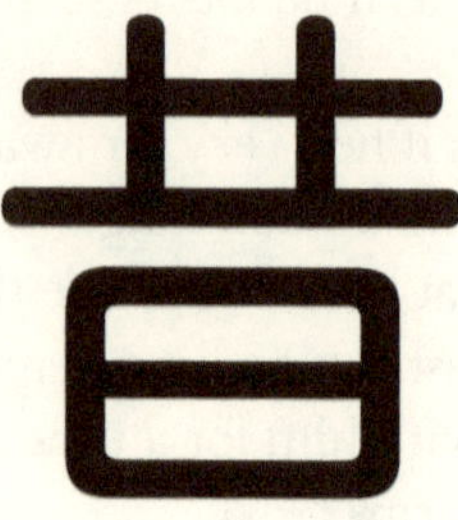

MY DORM HAD a large lounge on the ground floor that was often used by various student organizations for meetings and get-togethers. One time I was going back to my room after class, and there was a short Black woman with a crew cut standing at the front door with a large box of groceries in her arms, plus tote bags on her shoulders. The door was supposed to be unlocked for meetings, but maybe no one had gotten the memo. The box was heavy with two-liter bottles of soda and she had to prop it up on her knee, her combat-booted foot against the door frame as she tried to wave to someone inside.

"I got it," I said, and opened the door with my resident key.

"You're the best," she told me.

I responded to the praise by thinking I didn't deserve it. "Let me take one of your bags at least."

"If you really want to help, there's more in the car." She put the things down on a table in the lounge and then I followed her to a hatchback pulled up at the fire hydrant with its blinkers on. Between the two of us, we got the rest of the snacks and drinks inside. By then she had given me a long look, and vice versa. She wore her keys on a belt loop and her tank top showed a tattoo of an axe. Her voice held that soft note in it that could have been caution and could have been interest, but I didn't know which, when she asked, "So… you sticking around for this?"

I had to confess I didn't know what *this* was.

"Ah. It's a collaboration between the lesbian caucus, women's studies, and the gay student alliance, presenting a speaker." She spat out a name I didn't recognize, then added, with a note of vehemence, "I'm not staying."

"Oh? But—" But she had obviously worked hard to set things up.

"I will break my back for the community and for the right of everyone to speak their mind. But I don't need to listen to some victim-mentality crap about gender expression being oppression or that 'all sex is bad' bullshit." She went on like that a bit more, but I wasn't really absorbing what she said other than the fact that this wasn't a place she—or I—wanted to be. Something about her made my stomach flutter, and it flipped completely over when she added, "I thought you were a guy at first. Even with your hair."

"That happens to me a lot."

She grinned. "Hey, it even happens to me, even with these." She shifted her ample boobs with her hands to emphasize them. "Masculine energy or some shit. So what's your deal?"

I don't think I even stammered a response. I didn't have labels that fit—I had barely learned that there *were* labels, much less what they were. I might have said I was trying to figure it out, or maybe my panicked look of confusion said it for me.

"I gotta move the car before I get a ticket, but you want to grab dinner at the dining hall? Or a slice?"

"Um, sure."

"Wait here, I'll be right back."

While she was gone, I contemplated my hair. I had been letting it grow since I was 16 and my mother had approved because she approved of anything that seemed to indicate I was moving in a feminine direction. What she didn't know is that I carried two pictures in my wallet. One was of my father in his US Army uniform, his hair freshly shorn. The other was snipped from a magazine, of a kung fu movie star with his long hair up in a topknot. When I'd cut it out, I hadn't really thought about why. I had just felt I wanted—needed—to carry it with me.

I still wasn't ready then to think about why. So I fled before she could come back.

ARRIVE AT QUAN's back door slightly drunk on celebratory wine. Master Chang declared the peach done in mid-afternoon, and shortly after the entire household was plunged into a multi-hour feast. The cooks must've been anticipating it, or maybe they were able to get the whole roast birds—with smaller birds roasted inside!—from the local teahouse?

I amuse my drunken self with the idea that Chinese takeout is a tradition that dates back hundreds of years. The door is open. The screen door squeaks on its hinges a bit as I open it, but I tiptoe carefully through the heaps in the storeroom.

On the other side of the curtain to the front room I can hear Quan on the phone.

"I can't tell you where she is. I can only assure you she's working on retrieving it."

It takes me a moment to realize he's talking about me.

"I would give you her number, but she doesn't have one. I know, no cell phone. Crazy, right?" He chuckles and sounds far too amused. "I know, I know, you're exactly right. She's like some throwback to the nineteen-nineties, isn't she? Hang on, another call coming in."

His voice changes, astonishing me. "Hello, darling. Can you meet me tonight? Please say yes. Yes? Excellent. See you later." And he makes an actual kissing noise as a goodbye.

I tiptoe hurriedly back to the alley doorway and ring the bell like I haven't been inside. I've never heard him like that, ever, with anyone. Quan has a paramour? The whole world feels tipped on its side. Or maybe that's the wine.

He hurries me inside and puts the electric kettle on. "You smell like a hangover, Mei-Mei."

"It's not a hangover *yet*," I insist, sitting on the stool behind the counter and putting my hands over my eyes. "The sculptor finished today and it's been nonstop partying since."

"Oho, finished, you say? I'm surprised you came back without it, then." He sets a cup of tea down in front of me. The ceramic clicks against the glass countertop.

"The sculpting part is finished, but the part where it gets imbued with magical powers has to happen next," I tell him. Though it occurs to me suddenly, "I suppose the museum doesn't need it to be magical, though?"

Quan *hmphh*s softly. "If I were you, I would be careful around the court magician. It might be best to snatch it before it gets to him. After all..." he trails off. I open my eyes to see him frowning, one hand over his mouth.

"What's wrong?"

"Just remember sometimes magicians are gods in disguise.

Then again, so are beggars in the streets, so...never mind. I'm just being paranoid. If a god were going to expose you, there'd be nothing we could do about it." He looks into my bloodshot eyes. "A magician might still be tougher to deal with than a typical person, though."

"Okay, fine." I'm trying to think of some way to ask him about whether he's met someone and how does it work—if you're the kind of immortal who lives one long, unbroken life and then you fall in love with someone who doesn't? He told me he preferred not to get attached. Has he been hiding this person from me?

No, the relationship must be somewhat recent.

I pick the cup up carefully by the rim, but it has sat long enough that it's no longer very hot. I take a sip and gag a little. "What the hell is this?"

He spits out three syllables I can't parse without knowing what dialect he's speaking. "It's good for your liver," he adds.

I try another sip and nearly spit it out. I can't speak for my liver, but the intense bitter taste sobers me right up. *Gack.* "Quan, what am I going to tell Sandra?"

"About the peach?"

"No no no, I mean, personally."

"Did she ask you to marry her or something?"

Or something. "Well...she does seem really really interested in me."

"And you're not interested in her?"

"No! I *am* interested in her."

He looks me over like maybe I need a stronger dose of his hangover cure. "Then what is the problem?"

If I could answer that, I could probably solve it. "I don't know what she expects."

"Have you tried asking her?"

"Don't be ridiculous. If I ask her what she expects, she'll ask me what I expect."

"And what do you expect?"

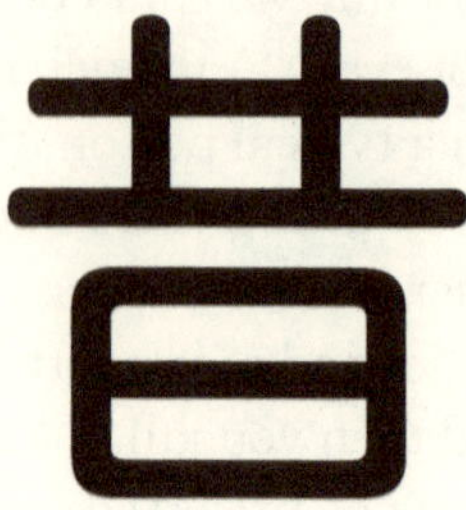

S EEING SKINNY DOU'S restaurant for the first time
since the day I'd fled there, a pang of dèjá vu rushed
through me so strong I almost had to sit down on
the sidewalk. No, not dèjá vu, because of course I actually
had been there before. It just seemed like something out
of a dream. I had brought Quan to the back alley by
the grocery and sent him around to check, afraid I'd
be seen. He'd confirmed she was there, and then as I
had promised, I delivered him back to his place before
returning on my own. In that upstairs room was the most
beautiful woman I had ever seen, and I hadn't even been
conscious enough of myself to know that's what I thought
until later. I had first arrived at this restaurant with a
head crammed full of women's studies and comparative
literature and politics, and none of it made sense. Then
each day Jin Jin's hands would transform me from an
overworked college student into something more elegant,
and I'd forget it all, at least for a while. As if every time I
went there, she would turn me into something new—no,
something *old*—while she herself never changed.

I looked at the window and I wondered if she could see me, but the reflected sky in the plate glass was as opaque as gold.

At the back of the restaurant, I could hear Skinny Dou yelling at the cooks through the open kitchen door.

I went through the doorway, but not into the kitchen. Now that I knew to listen to my heart, I could step right into her bedroom.

She sat at the window, her hair unbound and a comb idle in her lap, but as soon as I entered, she jumped up and ran to me. I took her hands in mine and I squeezed them.

"I'm sorry," I told her. "I didn't know. I didn't realize."

She just nodded, half-sad, half-elated.

"I'll take you back now. No more waiting."

I had planned on just whisking her off right that second, but she stopped me with a few quick words. She unearthed a silken dress from a wooden chest that covered her from throat to ankle. I helped her fasten it at the shoulder and down her back. Then she sat, spine as straight as a spear, in front of the mirror. I did her hair one last time, pinning it in place with slender, lacquered sticks.

We were silent all through it. I didn't have the words to try to explain anything—how I had been raised, why I had come to Skinny Dou's in the first place. How what I'd found at the restaurant wasn't the identity I'd been seeking. Or that for once, I wanted to bring a stolen treasure back where she belonged.

When she was ready, I took her hand. "Look." As we circled each other like waltz partners, the doorway to her room blossomed all around us like a thousand petals of a flower.

Quan said my gift, my power, was to go where I'm needed, or to go where I need to. Jin Jin tugged me, or maybe I tugged her, through the door and into a cobbled courtyard. My entire body began to beat like a drum, as if my heart filled my entire chest. Around us were grand buildings, the largest I'd ever seen in the ancient world, each upturned corner populated by an orderly menagerie of lucky animal carvings. They could be no less than Imperial.

Her breath caught as she pointed. Through a screen we could see into a shrine, and there he was, a young man in a tall headpiece, making his obeisance to his ancestors. Around him, candles flickered and incense burned, while he seemed to glow with a luminescence of his own.

I pulled her against a column, lest we be seen too soon, and she whispered her thanks to me over and over.

"Is this goodbye?" I asked, barely able to speak.

She leaned forward, her eyes crystalline with tears, and brushed her silken lips against mine.

And then she rounded a corner and was gone.

THERE'S NO FOLKTALE about the Dragon's Daughter where she dies of a broken heart, at least, none that I've heard. I keep telling myself that as I use Quan's phone to call Sandra. It rings and rings but before she or her voice mail can pick up, another call comes in. I see the name on the caller ID. *Charlie Ruykeyser.*

I answer it by reflex. "Hello, Quan's Antiques."

"Oh, hey." It's a man's voice. "Um, is he there?"

Yes, he's here and he's impatiently waving at me to hand him the phone. I do. Another quick, sweet, logistical conversation follows, about where they'll eat tonight, and then Quan hands the phone back to me, biting his lower lip.

I *have* to say something. "You're smitten."

"Utterly." He sighs. "It's been such a long time."

"I thought you didn't...dally with mere mortals. Or is he a vampire or something?"

Quan clucks his tongue and waves his hands at me. "Stop worrying about my relationships and worry about your own, eh?"

I dial Sandra again and this time she picks up right away. "Hi, it's Mei."

I can literally hear her smiling. "Mei! So great to hear from you! Are you...back in town?"

"Just for tonight," I say. "I wanted to let you know that I might have..." I hesitate to say *the peach* as if that might jinx it, "...results in the next twenty four hours."

"Wonderful." She lets out a weak sort of laugh. "And here I thought you were calling to say hello."

"Um, well..." I'm sure my face is red. Quan is pretending not to pay any attention. His eyes are on the crossword puzzle on the back of a folded newspaper, but he doesn't have a pencil in his hand. "Can I...could I see you tonight? While I have a chance?"

"Tonight would be great!" She sounds eager, speaking fast. "Do you want to come over and I'll cook? Or we could order in." Sandra clears her throat, but it doesn't slow her down one bit. "Or we could hit the place down the street. I mean, whatever you like. Or—"

"I'll just come over. Give me the address." If I didn't know better I'd think she's flustered. I didn't think Sandra Lim could be flustered. "It'll take me about an hour to get there, okay? I'm in Chinatown."

"Okay, an hour. Bye."

Was that a kissing noise at the end there? I'm not sure. I press the button and hand the phone back to Quan.

Frank curiosity is all over his face, his eyebrows practically climbing into his hairline.

"I don't know," I blurt in answer to his earlier, unanswered question. "I don't know what to expect. We've had two dates and I've been afraid to kiss her."

"That's not what I was going to ask about." He pours more hangover remedy into my cup and the scent of it alone makes me gag. "Before you go, let us finish talking about how you'll retrieve the peach. Or perhaps I should say, when. Is everyone there asleep, now?"

"Of course. They all drank even more than I did. No one will be going anywhere."

"Then isn't this the best time to make off with it? Assuming you can sober up enough to find your way back there." He frowns. "Or could you go to see Sandra, and then after that, travel back to the same moment when you left?"

I push the cup away. "I think if I tried *very* hard, I could return to the same moment when I left, but I'm really not sure. There might be unintended consequences. What usually happens is if I spend two days here, two days pass there, and vice versa. Just like opening the Gate always works best at sunrise and sunset. I forced it once...and that's when it went wrong."

He nods. "There are laws of nature at work, even if they're not the laws that govern most beings. Perhaps it is because you age, and it would be breaking the rules of your type of immortality if you didn't age at the same pace in all timelines."

"You think so?"

He shrugs. "Even your father has to bow to the laws of nature."

My head jerks up. "My *father?*"

"You *are* the Dragon's Daughter."

"So there's an actual Dragon out there? I thought that was just a...a...metaphor."

"Maybe it is. The Dragon is the very force of nature itself, all the powers of the sky and sea, as well as the spirit of the people. But you are no mere idea. Metaphors don't feel anxious, as you clearly do." He grins. "Go to your lover."

I put a hand on my hot cheek. "She's not my...I mean, we're still getting to know each other."

"Remember someday that you said so! It's proof of just how young you are."

I ARRIVE AT SANDRA's doorstep having traded my lowly rural scholar's jacket for my leather, my flat shoes for sneakers. The nighttime wind is biting. Has summer ended already? It's hard to keep my mind on the present when my thoughts are in the past. Maybe I should convince Master Chang to let me be the one to bring the peach over to Wang Gui, so it (and I) can conveniently disappear? Then I'll never have to find out if Wang Gui could be a danger to me.

Sandra lives in a renovated brownstone a bit of a hike from the train, on a street lined with old oaks. As I reach for the doorbell, there's a sudden tightness in my throat.

She opens the door and in an instant she goes from an abstraction in my mind to right there where I can touch her, reach for her. But I keep my hands in my pockets. "Hey," I say.

"Hey," she replies, ushering me inside. "Welcome to my place."

Before she can say more, a piercing whistle comes from the kitchen and she dashes away to take the kettle off the stove. I'm left staring at a painting in her living room, hung above a brick fireplace, that at first glance appears to be just an abstract black-on-black canvas, but as I move my head I notice a central focus of the swirling brushstrokes, a kind of figure...that could be a long-backed dragon twisting skyward in the updraft. Bare tinges of red and orange at the bottom of the canvas represent the edge of the clouds far below.

I travel where I'm needed, or where I need to be.

I find her in the kitchen, rummaging through a cabinet.

"Are you okay with herbal?" She pulls a few small, colorful cardboard boxes out. "*Ha.* Fitting. This one's called *Tension Tamer.*"

I'm just staring at her with my mouth slightly open. The box has printed on it a literal maiden in a red dress sitting on a dragon. A Western one, but still.

"Quan said you like tea."

That startles a laugh out of me. "Herbal's fine. I—"

"Great."

She stares back. We both start at the same moment to say, "I'm sorry," and we both laugh a little.

She forges ahead. "Look, I want to apologize before I lose my nerve. For scaring you off. I'm sorry. I know I come across as kind of intense."

"I was going to apologize for running away," I say. "But I guess if you're going to take the blame for it I'm off the hook."

Her laugh is more genuine, then. "I was afraid you weren't coming back." She pulls out two mugs from the cabinet over the stove and drops the teabags in, then pours the steaming water. Her back is to me while she fusses, still sounding nervous: "You said you had news about the peach. I...I have some news, too."

"Okay." I take a seat at the counter as she sets the mugs down.

She sits on another stool, facing me. Her hair is down, her glasses nowhere to be seen, and she's wearing skintight yoga pants, a crop top, and an oversize cardigan sweater. "I'm not supposed to say anything, but since I dragged you into this I thought it was only fair. The FBI is getting more actively involved."

"In looking for the peach?"

"Yes." She searches the ceiling for patience, but she's clearly out of it—with them, not me. "They've never given a rat's ass before about one of our artifacts going missing, but all of a sudden they're all over this one. I don't know what they think they're going to find, but they're going to pay Quan a visit. They don't know about you, yet. But your name is in the visitor register, so..." She exhales tiredly.

And if they try to search for me, they're going to find I don't exist. Or that I went missing decades ago. I'm going to be the most suspicious thing ever.

The tea is too hot to drink, and as far as I can tell it's doing nothing to tame the tension in the room. "Don't worry about me. I can just disappear."

She picks up her mug and looks at me over the top of it. "Mei Song's not even your real name, is it?"

"Depends what you mean by *real*," I say. "I'm adopted. All my names have been given to me."

Sandra thinks about that for a moment. "That's true of everyone, really, even if you're *not* adopted. It's not like we're born wearing a nametag."

Hm. "I guess in my case it's just more obvious there could have been a totally different me, a totally different life, if I hadn't been brought here as an infant."

I go where I need to. Where I'm needed.

She takes a careful sip. "You've always been a mystery to me. Maybe that's why I want to get to know you better."

"Because you don't like unanswered questions?"

"No, Mei." She looks into my face. "Maybe I'm making too many assumptions, but I grew up between worlds, stuck between the world my grandparents had left and the one my parents chose, stuck between American and not, all that. And you're one of the only people I've met who seems...who feels...like you're between worlds, too."

"The kids in your Mandarin class weren't like that?" I find myself asking.

She shakes her head. "None of them seemed to have the same level of angst as me over it, anyway. Maybe since they weren't mixed, they fit in better. With each other, at least." She rotates the mug in her hands. "I never fit in anywhere, and I get the feeling you don't either."

She is, of course, correct. "I've learned that I *can* fit in, but only with a lot of work," I say. "You know, I was about to say I only fit in when I'm pretending to be something I'm not, but I'm not sure that's true."

I don't really understand what I'm saying, but she nods like she does and says, "The thing is...when I'm in a room with you, your presence is...is everything." She blushes, but doesn't look away. "Like everything else disappears, and all I can see is you. And...it's probably way too early to admit this to you, because I'm probably going to just scare you off again, but I've never felt that way about anyone else before."

I decide maybe just saying what I'm feeling is the only reasonable course of action. "I want to kiss you so much my teeth hurt."

That is definitely a blush on her cheeks as she looks suddenly into the mug in her lap. "Are you afraid of commitment? One kiss doesn't have to mean—"

The only thing I'm afraid of right at that moment is knocking over scalding hot mugs of whatever as I reach across to cup Sandra's cheek and pull her toward me. Nothing spills and her mouth is hot and lush and herbal.

Her phone starts to ring from somewhere below and she breaks free to catch her breath and pull it from her cardigan pocket. "Oh. It's Quan."

She answers it and exchanges a few quick words with him, while I stand there still living in the previous moment, even as the heat dissipates from my lips.

She looks worried. "He wants to talk to you."

I take the phone and take in the news. The FBI agents have left him so rattled he can't remember which dialect to speak. But I get the gist. They're accusing him of the theft. He stammers something about Charlie as well. He doesn't have to explain why he's so upset. I understand this right away: if they make the accusations stick, this chance at happiness will be shattered. Unless I can do something about it.

And I can. I can bring back the peach.

"Don't worry, don't worry," I'm telling him. "I'll be back as soon as I can."

I hand the phone back to Sandra and she pockets it. Her eyes look red; she's holding back tears. "I know he's only tried to help. It's so unfair of them to try to pin the crime on him!"

"Why do they even suspect him?' I ask.

Sandra shakes her head again. "Because they're incompetent and he's convenient."

I stand up. "You know what would be really inconvenient for them? If you got a call from a mysterious stranger about this 'no questions asked' reward you're offering.'"

"You better be able to get it back."

"In that case, I better hurry." But I kiss her again before I leave, just in case I don't get another chance.

T HE FINAL TIME I saw my mother, I went to bring her something. I had taken a jaunt to find a gift for her and had been surprised to find myself in Hawaii. Honolulu's Chinatown seemed seedy and rundown, and a glance at the cars told me I'd hopped back into the mid-century, maybe 1969? That was unexpected, too. I didn't look too out of place for the time period, though my flannel shirt was too heavy for the weather. I wore a plain cotton T-shirt underneath, and jeans, and with my hair long, I supposed I could be taken for a hippie. On the street were plenty of faces that looked like mine, so I didn't stand out.

I was just starting to wonder if I should be looking for a gift shop or something, when a young couple stumbled out of a restaurant onto the street, nearly hitting me with the door and running right into me.

"Oh, whoops, so sorry!" the woman said as we bounced off of each other, her earrings swinging as she clung to her partner for balance. To him she said, "Dear, it's so bright out here I can hardly see!" She wore a flower-print minidress and he was in a military uniform. A shiver ran through me.

"Steady, dear. Yes, our apologies," he said, blinking at me, before adding, "Miss."

The shiver was recognition. I placed her perfume before her voice. The one she had worn when I was a small child.

These were my parents. I almost said *no worries* but people didn't say that back then. "Don't worry, I'm fine," I managed.

His arm circled her waist and he pulled her close, and she leaned in to press a kiss against his cheek, but he wasn't done speaking. "You're sure? You look a little stunned."

"Just surprised." I put my hand over my heart, which was hammering, but I smiled. In fact I could barely keep from smiling; they were so obviously and ridiculously smitten with each other—as well as a bit drunk. "You folks have a nice day now."

"You, too," they said simultaneously, and then broke out in laughter at themselves.

They walked down the sidewalk, weaving slightly as they leaned on each other, my mother chattering excitedly, my father beaming back at her. I did the math. This had to be shortly before his death in Viet Nam.

As they disappeared into a big restaurant on the corner, I noticed an earring sitting on the sidewalk at my feet. A single green teardrop. Jade, of course. I picked it up, thinking I should run after them. But as my hand closed around it, I realized, no, this is what I came for.

My trip to Ohio in 1992 took a lot longer, via Greyhound bus, which gave me a lot of time to think. I didn't remember ever seeing my mother that happy, like she had been a different person before becoming a widow. I had spent so long thinking of her as my mother—my entire life—that I spent the whole trip trying to remake my worldview. She would have been my age when they got married. They called each other *dear.*

When I reached my childhood home, the white siding had been repainted sage green, and the shutters were gone in favor of a white crown molding. I rang the bell.

I thought my mother was going to faint when she saw me. She came to the door with her hair in curlers, under a scarf. "What are you doing here? You didn't call!" She recovered quickly, though. "Don't just stand there, come in, come in!"

"I can't stay long," I told her as I followed her into the house. "Just passing through."

She turned in the foyer to stare at me. "You know, that's exactly what I've been expecting all along."

My mouth hung open, as her words kept coming, as if she had been rehearsing this speech in her mind for years. "I knew you were never going to stay. I sometimes hoped I might be wrong. But I always felt it, here." She pressed her fist to her chest. "That you were going to go back where you came from. Like I was only borrowing you. I tried, you know. I tried to be the best mother to you I could. I tried to make you at home here. But deep down my fear was that you'd n-never—" She broke off, voice wavering, and took a deep breath. "Tell me I'm wrong."

I shook my head. "You're not wrong." Part of me wanted to argue, to try to get her to understand that there were so many more reasons why I didn't fit there besides being adopted.

"You're here to say goodbye, aren't you."

There was no arguing when she was right. "Yes."

Her hand rested on her chest as she took another deep breath. "I've been preparing myself for this moment for so long, it doesn't hurt anywhere near as much as I thought it would."

It was the first time I could remember us feeling the same. We still hadn't gone any further than the entryway. "I didn't mean to be so out of touch, but—"

"Sweetie. It's not all you. It's me, too. That's what I learned in therapy." She laughed at herself a little. "I had a dream when you were little that you were a faerie child, and when you grew up you'd go back and leave the mortal world forever."

My skin prickled. That was so close to the truth.

"And every time I thought about it, I would have waves of anxiety. I thought, this is stupid: it was just a dream. But that was how I felt."

I thought about how shrill she used to get if she didn't like what I was wearing.

"After you left for college, I finally went to therapy because the anxiety was still there. And the therapist told me that somewhere, deep down, I still felt abandoned by your father. Even though it wasn't his fault, I still had that wound. Emotions don't have to follow logic, she said. And I told her I felt like he flew off to Asia and never came back, and some part of me feared that you would, too. And I'm sure my anxiety, which was really about him and me, and not you, probably—" She broke off again, steeling herself to say what she had to. "My anxiety got in the way of me loving you."

Flew off and never came back. I felt electric all over, almost like I did that first time I launched myself into the lucky red sky.

"The other thing therapy taught me is that a healthy goal for a parent is to raise an independent adult. Baby birds have to leave the nest. Be happy when they do." She exhaled again, and this time it was followed by silence, like she had run out of things to say.

"So, you're saying goodbye to me before I can say goodbye to you?" I asked.

"Well, I know I better say it now, because Lord knows if I'll get another chance. You do realize it's almost a year since I last heard from you?"

I did not in fact realize, since I didn't know exactly *when* I had landed until that moment. "I'm sorry. I've been traveling. And you're right. I did go back where I'm from." There was no way to tell her the truth, about being a reborn immortal or any of that. "So I came to say goodbye, and thank you."

"Thank me?"

"For being the best mom you could. And to give you something I picked up in my travels."

"Oh? What?"

I took the earring out of my pocket. She had given me a bracing dose of brutal honesty, and this was me doing the same: "I found it on the street in Hawaii and my intuition told me to give it to you."

I placed the earring in her hand. She stared at it for a moment, and then blinked until tears fell. But she smiled. "Sometimes the universe just gives you a sign."

We hugged.

And not long after, I flew away and never came back.

D AWN HAS NOT even broken yet as I stumble into the Chang compound, though the pink in the sky grows paler by the moment. The usual guards and maids and cooks are all fast asleep after the heavy revelry of the night before, and I wonder if maybe luck is on my side. Perhaps I can sneak the peach out of the workshop right now, and be gone before anyone even notices.

But as I slip into the courtyard that supplies most of the natural light to the work area, I find another figure standing under the eaves.

"Master Chang?"

"Ping, what are you doing up so early? There's no work to be done today." He steps out under the brightening sky.

"I...I wanted to see the peach one last time before it goes to Master Wang," I say with a bow. "After describing its beauty all night long, I scarcely believe my memory of it any longer."

"Ah, to be young again." He chuckles knowingly, as if I might have used my poetic descriptions to woo someone.

My fingers fly reflexively to my lip, wondering if there's some color there I'm not aware of. "I did spend some of the night ruminating about the nature of love, as well." Which was true.

"You may become a poet yet." He turns his face toward the scholar's stone at the center of the courtyard, but does not seem to focus on it. His eyelids seem heavy with either exhaustion or regret. "I'm sorry, Ping. But the peach has already gone to Wang Gui."

"Oh." I do nothing to hide my disappointment.

"Come, let us say our thanks to the gods and then have something to eat." He looks, like me, as if he has not slept, and yet his step is jaunty as he leads me out the gate and down the street. A cock crows as we make our way to a nearby temple. Outside those gates, a dozen carts have already formed a steamy, smoky, savory honor guard, as each side of the street is lined with food sellers. After he makes his obeisance inside, Master Chang buys us bird eggs hidden inside buns, meat wrapped in a wheaten cake, and a handful of other treats, all of which I carry back to the contemplation garden.

We each contemplate our own thoughts as we make our way through the food like a pair of barbarians, letting leaf wrappers and crumbs fall where they may. But then he speaks: "Ping, I sense you are thinking of leaving my household."

I lick sugar from my thumb. "My honored master is very perceptive."

He shakes his head in modesty. "You said you came to see the beauty of the gods made real by art. I merely note that your mission has been accomplished."

I stand and bow in agreement.

"Also..." He chuckles. "Your departure was as foretold as your arrival."

I pretend to be indignant when actually my skin is prickling like that time my mother struck so close to the truth. "I know what the future holds for me."

"Oh, do you? And does fortune smile on you?"

The best lies are the truth. "That may depend…upon her."

"Aha! I knew your musings over love could not be purely philosophical." He seems extraordinarily pleased with himself. "And does she know of your feelings for her?"

I'm blushing as hard as if we had drunk something stronger than tea. "Sometimes my feelings are so strong, I can't put them into words."

He nods. "Many are afflicted so. Indeed. The yearning one feels, the burning of longing when you are apart, that is the very fuel for the fires of my art."

"Is that why my honored master has never taken a wife? Because the fire might go out?"

His laugh is hearty, but tails off a bit pained. "When one's longing is quenched by the flood of desire flowing from the object of that longing, that is sweeter than the ripest fruit. But be cautious, boy, when you play with fire." His eyes grow shadowed as he looks away from me, and I wonder who or what he's thinking of. "Do not allow your own bile at being unrequited to quench it. You will stew forever in your own bitterness."

He seems to forget I am even there as he gets lost in his own thoughts, frowning.

"Master Chang? Has…has someone embittered my honored master?"

He laughs lightly this time, returning to the present. "No, no, my boy. There is one for whom I yearn, but I am content to stoke the fire a little longer." He gets to his feet suddenly. "I will say no more about it! Now, you should be on your way."

I bow deeply to him. "I will take my leave of you then, Master Chang. I will never forget you."

"Nor I you!" He laughs freely. "Now go." This time he hands me some coin, wrapped up in a bundle of cloth, a much more considerable amount than he dangled that day we first met. "That should be enough to let you travel back to your mother's side, or to stay in the city until you can take the exam. Perhaps even enough for a tutor."

"Thank you, honored sir." I bow low again, and when I straighten up, he has already disappeared into the house in a swirl of silk.

T HAT FIRST DATE with Sandra embedded itself in my mind in fragments. Each time I revisited it, it was like looking through a different window into the same house. Maybe it was the alcohol, or maybe it was drinking from the firehose of the experience of being with her, that meant my brain had to split it up into pieces to process them separately.

At one point we got on the subject of college, and I briefly forgot what century we were in and I said something about Pride Week at the school I went to. About how the gay student groups on campus used to put up a wooden pink triangle and then have to take turns guarding it overnight to keep it from being destroyed by homophobic frat boys.

"Pride *Week?* Only a week?" Her mouth and eyes were wide with surprise. "It was always Pride Month wherever I went. Even grad school."

I backtracked, trying to paper-over what I could not actually explain, "Oh, I think it was just that, you know, Pride Month is June, but the academic year is over by then, so we had a Week in the spring also." That sounded reasonable, didn't it?

She wrinkled her nose. "Sounds like the administration was less than fully supportive. That's the thing. We have anti-discrimination laws, but that doesn't compel homophobic institutions to change their attitudes, only their public practices."

"Yeah, we definitely got the bare minimum." It was starting to sink in just how big a leap in gay rights had taken place from my college days to hers—to now. I hurried to change the subject. "If you could go back and take one class now, what would it be?"

She leaned two fingers against her mouth as she thought about her answer, then took another sip of her sake-cocktail. "You know, there was a class I was interested in, on the Chinese Diaspora, but it always met at a time that conflicted with something I needed for my degree. I kept thinking, well, I should get the syllabus and just read the books for myself, but I never got around to it."

"Huh. I took one Chinese history class, in ancient history, but the main thing I remember is the guy went on and on about the size of the agricultural plots and the organization of the cities." Which turned out to be useful knowledge for me eventually, though I didn't say that. "I was kind of annoyed that he talked more about the architecture than the people. And he made us buy his own book as the textbook. I sold it back to the bookstore at the end of the semester!"

We laughed together and I felt so free in that moment, so unguarded. One part of me kept trying to go back into my shell, to keep my secrets, but it was like every time she opened herself to share a piece of what was in her mind with me, my inner self welled up reflexively to meet her.

And then I would retreat again, into my little pool of longing. At the time I told myself it was because it was hard to bridge the gap of the time between us, and that once I caught up to the way things were—*are*—then I would stop being so hesitant. But of course that was not my problem at all.

W ang Gui's home is not difficult to find. He has a sizable manor in the administrative district, nearly as fine as the provincial governor's, though not as large, and hemmed in on all sides by other buildings. It takes only a little coin to secure a small scholar's garrett on an upper story with a window facing one wall of his compound. When I crouch down, I can see through the slats of the shutter to the second floor of the house.

I lie down to sleep for the rest of the day, intending to take a closer look at sunset.

But as I lie there, I keep thinking about all that Quan, and Master Chang, and Sandra have said. Desire unrequited turns to poison. True love is eternal. I go where I'm needed, and where I need to.

Why was I brought forward into the twenty-first century? What I needed from Quan I could have gotten from him in 1992. But I hadn't thought about what *he* might need from me.

Was it the peach?

And what about me? What do I need?

At least now, in the twenty-first century, in America, Quan can marry Charlie. I can marry Sandra. It's possible. Even if that thought is slightly terrifying, we at least have the chance to explore whether that kind of love could grow between us. Whether we could be the kind of couple who buy statement piece art together.

We're also at a moment when those who are trying to take those rights away are surging up, too. I think about Sandra's fist banging her desk; she's ready to fight.

I think I am, too.

I give up on getting any sleep when two aspiring scholars who couldn't be any older than me start a loud argument in the courtyard outside. I crouch down and peek under the shutter of my window at them. Judging by their dress and their pretentious manner of speaking, they're from the eastern coast.

To my shock, Wang Gui himself appears at a second floor window and curses at them for the racket they are making.

One of them takes it in stride. "Honored master!" he calls upward. "Give me a subject and I will compose a poem so fine it will crush the soul of that unworthy cretin."

His rival, not to be outdone, calls up to the magician as well. "I, too, will compose a poem! Honored master, please be the judge of which of us is better!"

Wang Gui's beard is small and gray, and he tugs it as he considers the request. "Very well. But you must finish before the evening geng sounds from the drum tower or I will have you both expelled from the city. Both of you shall use the Lady Midnight style of verse."

One of them whimpers a bit at this pronouncement.

"As for your subject, hm." Wang Gui looks up as if searching for the answer in the sky, but then his gaze seems to settle directly at my shutter.

I swallow. It must be a coincidence. Surely he can't see me here.

"Ah, I know," he says. "Your subject will be the Nine Sons of the Dragon. Or any one of the nine."

It can't be a coincidence. He must sense I'm here.

I scramble backward through the doorway on my hands and knees and I am gone.

CRAWL DIRECTLY INTO the back of Quan's shop, and lie there, panting with fear.

"Are you all right?" He hurries over to me. "I've never seen you magic yourself right inside like that. Do you have it? Did you get it?"

I shake my head as I sit up. "Wang Gui...can sense me. I think." I describe to him what happened. "Soooo...who are the Nine Sons of the Dragon?"

"I will tell you over tea."

Of course he will. "Okay, real tea this time though, none of that hangover cure shit."

He laughs and goes to fill the electric kettle. I stand and brush myself off.

By the time he has the leaves steeped and two cups the size and shape of small tulips filled, I have doubts. I describe what feels like it could just be a coincidence, and yet… "Maybe it was all in my head."

Quan shakes his head. "Do not second-guess yourself."

Right. Trusting my intuition is supposed to be my power. "So do I have nine brothers out there?"

He ponders a moment, amused by the question. "There are nine mythological animals that guard buildings and palaces. You've seen them, right?"

"I can't say I've really paid them much attention." There was probably a lecture on them in that long-ago class, and I probably slept through it.

He gives me a sorry look and then digs around in a display case holding a dusty collection of books and papers. He pulls out what appears to be some Beijing governmental tourist propaganda, with glossy color photos of the Forbidden City. "Here we go." A colorized photograph of the roof guardians is labeled in Chinese. I recognize some of the characters. Dragon, for one.

Quan points to them one by one. "This one is half-dragon and half-fish and will help protect the building from fire. This one is half-dragon and half-lion." And so on down the line.

I frown. "If all the Dragon's sons are half-dragon and half-something else, what am I half of?"

Quan looks me up and down. "Human, I'd say?"

I can't tell if he's joking. I point at the photo. "And who's the guy riding the chicken?"

"He's the Immortal Riding a Rooster, of course!"

"Of course…?"

Quan rattles off the name in a few different dialects and all boil down to the same thing: *Immortal Riding a Rooster.* "Some say the rooster is a phoenix in disguise.

Some say the Immortal was an emperor's brother who was made into an eternal roof guardian as a punishment for his oversized ambition to be in high places." He chuckles. "The life of an immortal isn't guaranteed to be happy, after all."

And, as I'm getting used to, there isn't ever just a single story. I sip the tea and it tastes almost like incense, fragrant and smoky, sweet without being sugary. "Speaking of immortal happiness, I have to say...I'm happy you found Charlie and all, but...Quan, what are you going to do when he ages and you don't? I thought you said you didn't get attached." A sudden thought occurs to me, and a pang of fear strikes. "Or have you decided it's time to move out of Chinatown and let yourself age after all?"

He closes his eyes regretfully for a moment, but only a moment. "Mei, I haven't been totally honest with you."

"Oh?"

"I have a confession to make." He shivers a little, but he forges ahead. "It wasn't bigots or art thieves who took the peach from the Met."

It all makes sense suddenly—his oversized concern about it, his change of heart about getting into relationships, why the FBI are suspicious about him—it's all because: "Quan! *You* stole the peach!"

He cringes like I just flogged him or something. "Yes, I did."

"No wonder the FBI is after you! Do they have evidence?"

"They wouldn't tell me what exactly, but it sounds like they have something." He sighs. "I know. I know. I was foolish, but love will do that to a person." He rests his hand on his cheek though, looking much less distressed than I might expect for someone who might have just blown up his entire safety net.

"You gave the peach to Charlie."

He nods. "And the legends were true."

"You made Charlie immortal?" I'm aghast. "How long have you known this guy? Are you really ready to spend your eternal life with him?"

He clucks his tongue. "Listen to you! Like some auntie! You think I just met him last week? Mei, I've known him longer than you. Sometimes...sometimes if it's nurtured slowly over a long period of time, love can be even sweeter and more enduring than when it burns hot and fast, like when you are young." He fusses for a moment. "Ha, listen to me trying to be wise. It only took, what, 1200 years for me to learn it or something?"

Oh. Which means... "The reason I came to the 2020s is to save your ass!" I wonder how many years they've known each other. Long enough, I suppose. "I guess for true love, though, it must be worth it, right? The peach would've just remained stone if you weren't really meant for each other."

"My thinking exactly." Another pang of bliss crosses his face as he lifts the cup to his mouth, as if he's remembering the taste of the fruit. Then he looks at me seriously. "You see why it's so important that you retrieve it."

"Does Sandra know?"

"That I'm immortal?"

"*That you took the peach.*"

"No." He grimaces. "And I think to tell her one would be to tell her the other. What about you? Does she know?"

"No." I find myself suddenly queasy with shame. How could I ever expect a relationship to blossom between us when she literally doesn't know the single most important thing about me? I've kept everything of myself from her. I've been telling myself it was because I couldn't tell her what I didn't know myself, but I realize now that I've been approaching it backwards. "Let's go tell her now."

"What? *Right* now?"

"No time like the present," I say. "We'll both confess what we've been hiding. You owe her that much at least."

He grimaces, shame-faced. "All right. But this doesn't solve the question of how to get past Wang Gui."

"We can talk on the way. Come on."

H E CALLS HER when we come up out of the train and they argue briefly. They both agree that there's a chance that the FBI suspect Sandra herself, or that they would if they find Quan at her apartment. But they can't agree on whether Quan is likely being surveilled, if they have someone staked out at her place, or what.

I think they're being paranoid, but it doesn't matter. "Tell her to close all her curtains and shades," I say.

"She says they're already shut. She doesn't like anyone being able to see inside."

"Perfect. Tell her to sit in the living room and keep her eyes on the doorway to the kitchen."

Quan's jaw goes slack for a moment as he realizes what we're about to do. "Sandra, did you hear that?"

I can hear her reply: "Yes, I did. I'm sitting now."

I don't even give Quan a chance to hang up. We're walking past a takeout joint with red-tasselled lanterns hanging on the outside of the door. I hook my elbow in his, think about the painting on Sandra's brick mantelpiece, and step through the doorway.

My timing is slightly off, or maybe Sandra's is. I hear the gasp from behind us rather than in front as I expected, followed by the sudden shriek of the tea kettle. The whole place feels full of steam to me as I whirl around to face her.

She doesn't take her eyes off of us, but she kills the flame under the kettle and the sound trails off.

"Um, hi," I say.

"Hi." Her gaze slides from me to Quan, an accusation forming on her face.

"Sandra," he says, wringing his baseball cap in his hands. "What if I told you that everything you wrote about in your thesis was true? You'd be happy, wouldn't you?"

She looks even more suspicious. "Depends on your definition of *happy*. Or maybe your definition of *everything*."

I sigh. "You were supposed to be sitting on the couch."

"I thought I had time to make the tea before you got here." She's frowning. "How did you get here so quickly from the train station?"

Quan's knuckles are white around his poor, abused hat. "Didn't you see us appear? Like...like..." He looks at me for help.

Before I can find the right words, she just nods and reaches for the kettle, which is still making some pinging noises. "Tea? Maybe we should sit in the living room after all."

I usher Quan into the living room and we sit side by side on the low, black suede loveseat beside the painting. Sandra sets three steaming mugs down on the coffee table.

Quan and I look at each other. "You first," I say.

"I don't think either of us should be first," he counters. "Our stories are intertwined."

Sandra just cradles her mug, waiting for us to explain.

"Here, I'll tell her about you, and you tell her about me." I pick up my own mug. Smells like mint and honey and maybe ginger? "Do you know the story about the fishseller who swallowed the pill of immortality?"

"Yes." She blows on the mug. "I've heard that one."

"Well, you're looking at him. And that one about the peach turning real if true lovers shared it?"

She looks back and forth between us again. "You mean you're both immortal, now?"

Quan waves his hands, suddenly alarmed. "No no, don't get the wrong idea. Sandra, I'm so sorry. I had Mei get that Five Dynasties bowl for you because I knew I...I knew I was going to need the peach myself." He snuffles hugely, like he's trying to keep from bursting into tears by just sucking everything back into his head. "For someone else! I...I proposed to someone. I know how it sounds. But I've been alone for a very long time. And I couldn't resist the chance to be not-alone for, for, also a very long time."

"His name's Charlie," I blurt. "He seems very nice."

Sandra puts a hand over her eyes for a moment. "I'm sure he is." She looks back at Quan, and her expression is softly amused. "So you're telling me the fairy tale about the fishseller is true. And so is the one about the peach and true love."

"Yes!" He bites his hat as he sobs in relief. "I'm so sorry, Sandra. I didn't mean to make so much trouble for you."

She takes a careful sip from her mug. "So...which other stories are true?"

"Oh, lots of them," he enthuses, rattling off a few as she nods at each one, until he gets to, "And the one about the Dragon's Daughter?"

"I don't think I know that one." She frowns. "I know about the Dragon's nine sons, though."

"Why does everyone know about the Dragon's nine sons but not about me?" I huff, annoyed.

Sandra lifts an eyebrow. "Sexism, probably."

"What about the Emperor's Eternal Concubine?" I try. Quan raises his eyebrows a little at my addition of *Eternal* but says nothing.

"Nope, don't know about her either." Sandra can't help shifting into lecture mode, and I can't say I mind. I do love listening to her voice, and her thoughts. "I'm sure most of what I know was translated to English by colonialists who applied their own bias to which stories they considered important. You know we might not even have *Mulan* if Maxine Hong Kingston hadn't written a book about her?" She stops herself and looks at me over the top of her mug. "But what does this have to do with you, Mei?"

Quan says it in Mandarin first, then English. "The Dragon's Daughter can fly anywhere the lucky red sky touches."

"Including Zhili in the year 1483," I add. "I mean, 4180. You were right, by the way, about Chang Kuo-Jung."

She bites her lip to contain her excitement. "He's the artist?"

I nod and she makes a tiny pumping motion with her fist. "I knew it! They wouldn't let me put it on the plaque but...I knew it."

"I saw him make it myself," I say. "And I think I can get it from the court magician, Wang Gui. But I'll need help." I nudge Quan. "To redeem himself for stealing it, Quan's going to come with me."

He groans. "*Me?* How?"

"I need a diversion so I can snatch the peach while Wang Gui's busy. Because he can sense I'm not a normal mortal." I suddenly realize something else Sandra needs to know. "I'm not the kind of immortal Quan is. I age like a normal human. And then I'm reborn, or something, I guess." I elbow him. "Right?"

"Right," he says, moaning in fear. "I can't go with you, Mei. Charlie and I are so close to having our dream come true! I can't risk it."

"But you owe Sandra, and me!"

He sighs. "I know. But Mei, if Wang Gui can sense you're immortal, he'll be able to sense I am as well. I can't be the one."

Sandra sips from her mug. "You're ready to settle down with him—with Charlie, I mean—for literal eternity? How long have you known this guy?"

"You, too? Augh, you're both like aunties already." He hides his face in his hat for a moment. "I'm literally a thousand years older than you!"

I tell her, "He's already warned me we're going too fast, by the way."

"That is *not* what I said." Quan is clearly fed up with being teased. "I said...when love is nurtured slowly over a long period of time, it can be more enduring than the hot, fast kind. I didn't say the hot, fast kind is *bad*." He looks back and forth between Sandra and me.

"I think Mei was being sarcastic," she says, never taking her eyes off me.

I smile because she's right.

She sets her mug on the table. "So, you can't just wait until Wang Gui is out of town, or busy or something?"

"Not if we want to get the FBI off Quan's back."

"You need something that will be not just a distraction, but something that draws his magical focus," Quan adds. "Otherwise, he'll sense you. Something like getting him to work on a charm."

I set my own mug down and notice Quan hasn't touched his. *Ha.* "I could pay someone to make a request for a charm?"

"Or I could go with you." Sandra folds her hands. "Right? Assuming you can bring a mere mortal with you?"

"There's nothing mere about you." I really want to crawl across the low table and kiss her until we can barely breathe, but I'm not about to do that with Quan sitting right there.

"I have the perfect idea," he says. "You know how crossing water changes your luck?"

"It does?" Sandra and I say simultaneously.

Quan shakes his head and prepares himself to explain.

"DO I LOOK all right?" Sandra turns carefully in front of the full length mirror I'm holding in the narrow path in Quan's store room.

I can only nod. With her hair done this way, in silken finery...she doesn't look like Jin Jin at all, but the reminder is so strong that my throat is frozen.

Quan hands her some papers—letters to Wang Gui, and some others made to look like official documents of the era—and she slips them inside her jacket sleeve.

"You look stunning," I finally manage.

"I'm more worried about how I'm going to sound. It's been ages since I actually spoke Mandarin." She hides a nervous laugh behind one hand in a gesture that is so Chinese I almost do a double-take. "Last time I used it regularly was when I was working on my masters, what, five years ago?"

Quan adjusts the small headpiece atop Sandra's hair. "Mei just pretends to be from some other province and no one bats an eye that her grammar and pronunciation are atrocious."

"Hey! I'm not that bad!" I slide the mirror between the wall and a stack of crates where it normally hides. "How about me, do I look ready to go?"

I'm in a slightly nicer outfit than usual, to look more like a scholar than a common laborer, my jacket black instead of blue, with accents in green and yellow thread. He looks me over as usual, but I'm really wondering, of course, what Sandra thinks. She's never seen me like this.

"You look like an extra in a Jet Li movie," she says.

"She looks a lot like I did in 4180," Quan adds with a laugh.

"Quit it. Let's go." I hold out my hand for Sandra and she takes it. Hers is clammy.

"So how does this work?"

"It's easier to show than explain. Just...make sure you don't let go." I lead her into the alley. Dawn is breaking. We've been up all night talking and plotting. A garbage truck bangs and screeches to a stop at the far end of the alley, signaling that morning has officially begun.

We are gone before the men can even swing down off the truck. The alley we appear in will someday be in Hebei. I've been here before, behind the marketplace.

It's morning here, too, the clamor for provisions just beginning. "Looks like breakfast time," I say. "I'll take you to a teahouse where you can wait until you hear back from Wang Gui."

"Good plan," she replies, but her eyes are wide with wonder. One hand touches her headpiece tentatively to make sure it's still there.

At the teahouse it is not difficult to find a boy who will take a letter to Wang Gui for her. Sandra settles into her role quickly, bossing the staff around until they have seated her in a chair appropriately high such that her silks will remain up off the floor, while I—obviously her subordinate—sit beside her on a much lower stool.

I get into the act and call for my mistress's favorite to be brought: the buns with whole eggs inside them.

As we sit there passing the time, eating the buns and sipping a tea that tastes almost like roasted almond, Sandra whispers to me, "The dim sum place in Queens I like is never going to seem authentic again."

I have to hold back a laugh at first, but my thought is serious. "But, you know, it's all authentic to me."

She nods. "My thesis would've been so much easier to research with your help."

The bun is sweet on the outside, but rich and salty inside. "You know, when we're done with this, we could explore other times and places. More papers for you to write and publish."

"Maybe...?" She watches two men—one pushing and one pulling—maneuvering a wooden cart of lumber down the street. "Or maybe I just want to go back and find out the real story behind some of the things we don't know. Like...there are a few Tang Dynasty artists who modern scholars suspect may have been women in disguise. Wouldn't it be interesting to find out?"

The boy from earlier comes running back in, waving the reply in his hand. He clearly expects something more from us, though I am certain Wang Gui would have already paid him. I give him an egg bun and a cuff on the ear and he seems pleased as he runs away.

We are in luck—of course we are—Master Gui is in residence and he will grant her an audience that afternoon. Sandra wants to know how we'll know what time it is and I explain the tower with the drums and gongs.

Sandra is posing as the wife of a wealthy seafaring merchant, and she is here to ask for a blessing of some kind that will keep him safe when on an ocean voyage. While he's making the blessing, Wang Gui should be focused enough that he won't sense me sneaking through his house.

At the appointed time, she marches up to Wang Gui's front door while I sneak back to my scholar's garrett.

I slip into a bit of a trance, to center myself before making the jump, and behind my closed eyes I can see a flow of energy, a single funnel spiraling down from the sky. It must be Wang Gui invoking the spirit to create the charm. Time to move.

As I step into the Gate, the peach pulls at me. I step out of a doorway on the upper story of Wang Gui's house.

His chanting booms from below. Good.

The peach sits upon a small pillow on a worktable scattered with scrolls and writing. Although only a little bit of the afternoon sunlight filters into the workroom, the peach itself is luminous.

It's as beautiful as I remember it. Worthy of poetry, should I ever be moved to write any. The way it fits in my hand is almost sensuous. Master Chang could have made this stone look like any peach he wanted, but he chose this. I am struck by how every tiny decision made by the sculptor along the way was meant to embody an emotion and then to convey it. If humans can understand each other's gestures, is it such a leap that they could read each other's brushstrokes? Or other artistic endeavors?

"Put that down."

I clutch the peach to my chest as I whirl around. Wang Gui himself fills the doorway.

"I've been waiting for you to show yourself," he says. His hands are hidden inside his sleeves, which are long and black and embroidered with dragons.

I say nothing. He's blocking the way to the hallway, but not the door into the next room. Could I do it? Could I just dive through there and would it work? I let my eyes go soft as I prepare myself but my breath catches. Wang Gui becomes a being made of lightning, his shape defined by the thunderclouds around him.

"Give that to me," he says.

I shake my head, even as my mind races, trying to think of what to say to him. I settle on, "I need it more than you do."

When he laughs, the whole room shakes like it's trying to contain a thunderclap. "Oh, do you now? And which of my sons are you?"

I am struck silent again. This is not just any god in disguise. This is the Dragon.

And he doesn't know me. "Can't you tell?"

He snorts and a gust of wind kicks up the papers on the table. "When you wear a human shape, your origins are concealed, just as mine are. But that is all it is: a skin that can be shed."

"What if I'm part human and part dragon?"

He looks puzzled. "All the people are part human and part dragon."

This has to be a translation mistake, I think, but I'm just trying to stall him until I can get to the doorway. "You should give me the peach."

"Why? It belongs to Kuo-jung." The Dragon chuckles like the rumble of a far-off storm. "What do you know of it?"

"I know he intends to give it to…to someone he loves. To test if their love is true." I remember something Sandra said, five hundred years in the future. "But I know that the peach will remain stone." So either Master Chang's intended love was not true…or he never worked up the nerve to give it to them. "I worry it will break his heart."

The Dragon looks me up and down. "Are you Suanni? I know you are wise, but not prophetic."

"I am not Suanni. I have seen the future," I say. "Don't let poor Master Chang suffer. The disappointment will turn him bitter. Poison will run through his veins. I should take the peach."

"Pulao? Only Pulao would be so kind. Jiaotu? Only Jiaotu would work so hard to keep others from harm."

The fire in his eyes has tempered now, from anger at my affront, to curiosity. "I fear you are right and that no good will come of this peach."

"I am not Pulao or Jiaotu." I rock back and forth on my toes, preparing to leap for the door. "If you know no good will come of it, why would you agree to charm the peach for Chang Kuo-jung to begin with?"

"You are too young to understand." He swallows, his lips pressed in a thin line. "I have grown unusually fond of him. I find I can deny him nothing."

Oh, my. "*You're* in love with Chang Kuo-jung?"

He nods, an amused smile curving one side of his mouth. "An artist, a poet, and one of the few virtuous, good-hearted men I have met of late. Do you not think him worthy?"

"He's quite worthy," I stammer. "But is he not also in love with you?"

The Dragon snorts like a disbelieving wind, as he is apparently not an all-seeing god. "Not currently. But I think he would come around, given time, and time I have plenty of."

I try to hold my mirth in check. Humans and dragons alike can be inscrutable, apparently.

The Dragon's eyebrows descend like thunderclouds. "The peach, however, complicates things. Whomever he grants it to will surely be charmed by his regard, and I will be left waiting, perhaps until he is too old to appreciate my attentions. Or, as you say, too embittered by the experience."

I think of my mother's words about anxiety getting in the way of love. "But you would charm the peach for him, anyway? And if he found true love with another, you would be happy that he was happy?"

"Yes." The Dragon's eyes narrow, as if he is trying to see right through my flesh and bones to the chunk of jade I'm still clutching. "Only a man of such virtue would believe in *true love*."

"So true love is a myth?"

"That is not what I'm saying. So much of what we experience as love is just this." He tugs at his silk robe. "But our costume is not who we are. Neither is our skin. How can there be true love if no one dares to leave their true heart exposed?"

Indeed. Isn't that the exact thought I had when I realized I had to tell Sandra about myself? I bow to show I agree.

"What of you, my child? If I let you take the peach, to whom will you give it? That fiery flower you sent to distract me?"

Sandra! My heart leaps, both to think of her, and the idea that he may let me take the peach after all. If so, I feel chagrined at having been so rude as to try to steal it. "I do not know if what is growing between her and me is true love but I intend to let it grow as it will."

He chuckles. "Ah, but then, if you give her the peach, is it a blessing or a curse? If it remains stone, or turns to the fruit of immortality?"

I freeze like a statue. Shit. He's right. I need the peach to remain jade, or—relationship stuff aside—we'll just be in the same mess all over again. "Um, I would prefer to let my love for her grow without the burden of prophecy," I say. "I want to, as you say, show her my whole heart. I want to be fully honest."

"Fully honest, hm? But you cannot be my son Bi An, for Bi An is so law-abiding that you would never have dared to steal from me in the first place." He seems amused by his own guesses. "If you are going to be fully honest, then you must tell me what you plan to do with the peach."

Fine. The truth is easier than trying to invent something. "Where I come from, the people are having arguments on the nature of love and what kind of love to allow. And there is a museum of art and culture. And we believe this to be the greatest work of art about love that has ever been created."

"And you hope that art will tame the arguments?"

"Quite the opposite. Art should *inspire* both critical thinking and move people's emotions. If it ends the arguments, it will be because compassion and good sense won out." I hold the peach up so that we can both admire it. "Am I being foolish?"

He smiles with his eyes. "It is the privilege of the young to be foolish. I told you the peach would be troublesome."

"I will need to find a way to give it to her without invoking the charm."

"That will be simple, my child. *I* will give it to her. Did you bring her here to ask if I see virtue in her? If so, yes, but this is an unusual way to ask for my blessing."

I bow low, again, clutching the peach to my breastbone. "So you'll give it?"

"My blessing, or the peach?"

"Both."

He sighs. "Yes. But heed my warning. Nothing, not charms nor poems, can compel one to love. True love can only be built, like a house, with four hands placing new timber day after day."

I bow again. "I'll remember that. What are you going to tell Chang Kuo-jung?"

"About the peach, or about my feelings for him?"

"Both," I say again, letting myself smile.

"Nosy child." His hand emerges from his sleeve and he strokes his beard. "I will tell him that when I called on the spirit to charm the peach, it blackened and turned to a cinder, because of how he has been so unaware of my ardor for him."

That makes my smile even wider. "So you'll tell him how you feel?"

"If you are ridding me of the troublesome peach, then yes." Thunder rumbles overhead, but he moves aside and gestures for me to step into the hallway. "She is waiting for us." Then he holds out a hand for the peach.

I place it into his palm and he gives me an approving nod in return.

He leads me to the audience parlor below, much grander than Master Chang's. This room is paneled with finely carved wood, and in niches along the wall are various works of art, paintings, scrolls of poems, statuettes, and so on. Sandra sits next to a table scattered with tea things, watching a monkey perform tricks. The monkey's trainer turns and bows to us as we enter—the monkey does, too—and then they leave. Sandra stands expectantly, eyes darting to me with worry.

I try to smile, but I'm feeling so many different things I don't know if it comes out reassuring or not. It might just be a crazed grimace.

The Dragon produces a measure of black silk with a flourish and then tucks the peach inside, wrapping it like an egg, before handing it to Sandra. She takes it with both hands and a bow. "Thank you," she says.

I cross the room and take her hand in mine. "We should go."

The Dragon clears his throat. Outside, a rainstorm has begun pelting down. "Before you go, child, tell me one thing in return."

I step up to the polished wood of the threshold. Outside the water pours down like curtains. "What could I possibly tell you?"

He stands in the very middle of the parlor, centered, like an immovable pillar, but for all his armor, his voice still breaks when he asks, "Do you know whom it is that Chang Kuo-jung holds dear in his heart? He clutches it as tightly to him as you did that lump of jade in your hand."

There is, of course, only one person I've ever seen Master Chang look happy beside, only one in whose presence he forgets all others. It amuses me that I have seen it, but he has not. "As tightly as you clutch your own secrets?" I ask. "I am certain he has no idea you feel for him as you do."

"Yes, and?"

I'm not a very good poet off the cuff, really, but I try: "Curtains work in both directions." I shake my head. I can do better. I try again: "A cloud obscures the sun from the land, but also the land from the sun."

His eyes widen. "Are you saying—?"

"I thought dragons were supposed to be quick-witted and observant? You'll have to tell him yourself to find out," I say, and then I pull Sandra behind me and we dash through the doorway.

We land in some other alleyway, it's probably New York, and it's pouring rain here, too, we're getting utterly soaked, both shrieking from joy and the cold of the sudden deluge. I pull Sandra to me by the waist and rather than try to remember what language we're supposed to speak or whether we are wearing the right clothes I decide instead this is the right moment to let my tongue cleave her lips apart.

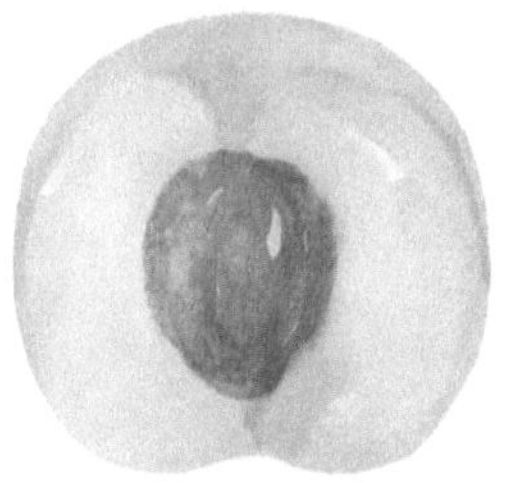

ACKNOWLEDGEMENTS

THANKS FIRST OF all to Joselle Vanderhooft, who first put the bug in my ear to finish the half-written draft of this story that had been languishing on my computer. Later, that draft doubled in size, so double thanks to beta readers Kristin Osani, Claire Light, Emma Mieke Candon, and Charlie Jane Anders. I should also thank Shariann Lewitt and Max Gladstone who both had to listen to my struggles while I wrestled this one to the ground. Bolin Zhang and Tse Wei Lim also put in their two cents (or should I say two qián?). A shoutout to Nancy Bereano of Firebrand Books, along with Michele Karlsberg and Aren X. Tulchinsky, who were the first to publish a story about the Dragon's Daughter back in the 1990s. And to dave ring, for taking such care in publishing this one. I'm dedicating this book to my first writer role model, my aunt, Maureen Brady, who continues to inspire with her writing that delves into family cultural roots. And love, always, to corwin.

ABOUT THE AUTHOR

A bigender biracial bisexual who spans the gamut of genre and gender, Cecilia Tan is known as a pioneer in queer science fiction and fantasy publishing. Inducted into the Saints & Sinners Hall of Fame in 2010 for her contributions to LGBTQ literature, Tan was recognized as the founder of Circlet Press as well as for her long fiction career. The author of over 100 short stories in publications ranging from *Ms. Magazine* to *Asimov's, Sunday Morning Transport* to *Best American Erotica,* and over 30 books and novels including the Magic University series, *Daron's Guitar Chronicles, The Prince's Boy,* and *The Velderet,* she has also been recognized with the RT Book Reviews Career Achievement award and many others. "ctan" (see-tan) as she is commonly known accepts all pronouns but uses she/her for society's convenience. She recently published a paranormal urban fantasy with BDSM elements entitled *Bound by the Blood,* and she might be working on another book with dragons... if she doesn't get distracted wanting to write a very gay chess rivalry novel. Find out more at CeciliaTan.com.

ABOUT THE PRESS

Neon Hemlock is a Washington, DC-based small press publishing speculative fiction, rad zines, and queer chapbooks. *Publishers Weekly* once called us "the apex of queer speculative fiction publishing" and we're still beaming. Learn more about us at neonhemlock.com and on social medias at @neonhemlock.